Chilled to the Bones

Linda Lee Kane

TSL Publications

First published in Great Britain in 2023
By TSL Publications, Rickmansworth

Copyright © 2023 Linda Lee Kane

ISBN: 978-1-915660-53-4

Cover : Trevor Smith

Dedicated to
my
family

Prologue

ON A WARM SUMMER afternoon, construction workers wiped the sweat from their brows as they sat on self-made benches of five-gallon paint cans to take their last break. The main crew had already left for the day, and a lack of supervision gave them some flexibility. Adding an extension to the old Ward Melville High School was a big job and hard work. Dust and dirt filled the air as they watched Warren manipulate the backhoe's huge scoop. None of the men were particularly anxious to finish any too quickly. Heavy concrete forms had to be moved into place before the day was done, and they were already tired.

The backhoe stopped, and conversation ceased momentarily to see why. Warren hung his body out the window, his neck stretched forward as he clung to the door.

"What's up, man?" Joe hollered. "Something in your way?"

"Yeah, there's something in my way all right. I've uncovered a pile of bones."

"Bones? What kind of bones?"

"Bones, human bones with a skull."

"Oh, my God!" the workers yelled in unison as they scrambled off their paint buckets and slid down the embankment of the hole Warren was peering into.

"Should we move them?" Joe asked.

"Well, I can't dig with them there," was all Warren could muster.

Trevor picked up a long tree root and nudged the skull. It rolled over, and empty sockets stared back, vacant and weathered by time. The backhoe had cast the rest of the bones adrift in the dirt. They were a strange dirty tan color, and the hinges of the arms and legs were bulbous. He leaned down to investigate them more closely.

Several hundred years and the right soil conditions for the fungus that had settled in the buried bones propagated a walking terror. Trevor was chosen as the new host for that terror. What was left of the other workers' bodies was disposed of, and darkness fell.

Chapter 1

"HEY, DEALER, YOU UP for a ride to the grocery store?" Mom had a way of picking the most inopportune moments to run an errand.

"Sure, Mom, let me just finish talking to Catherine about school tomorrow, and then I can come."

For some odd reason, death entered Dealer's mind. She'd never thought much about dying. It seemed inconceivable, but then most teenagers believed they were invincible. Maybe that's why they tried stupid things, like jumping off a cliff when they didn't know how deep the water was or passing a ball between cars. The concept came and went. Little did she know it was a foreshadowing of things to come in her life over the next few months.

The silence broke again. "Okay. I'll be down in the car waiting. Why don't you think of something you might like to have for dinner tonight?"

"Mmm," came the response; Dealer paid little attention to what her mom said. She was more focused on what Catherine Barry was saying about the big pep rally scheduled during school tomorrow.

Trivial matters attended to, Dealer ran out her bedroom door, turned the corner, and almost collided into a woman wearing a black lace dress. She seemed to have come out of the wall as she stood in front of it, gazing at the girl who appeared to be in a hurry. Long curled black hair hung limply over thin shoulders that carried a taller than average frame. She smelled of lavender, and though Dealer could see her vividly, she knew it was an impossibility because she could see right through her.

Frightened, Dealer ran down the flight of stairs, completely jumping over the last four steps to the landing. She regained her footing and raced out the front door. The screen door slamming behind her startled her, and she tripped over her feet and nearly fell.

"What's going on, Dealer?"

Feelings of stupidity and nervousness grabbed Dealer as she fumbled for a response. "Nothing, Mom. I just thought of something I wanted to eat for dinner and got excited to tell you." The last thing she wanted to do was admit that she had just seen a ghost. Her mom would think she was crazy, and then a long discussion would ensue that would get neither of them anywhere.

The air had a chill to it, and Dealer found herself hugging her arms. Grabbing onto the handle of the car door, she slid into the front seat of her mom's beat up yellow Volkswagen. The seat springs squeaked and made such a grating noise that she couldn't help but squirm. It crossed Dealer's mind that the recovered seats in a leopard pattern should disgust her, but somehow they were okay.

"Dealer, make good grades, and this car will be yours," she heard her mom boast. It was her mom's first car, and she loved it to this day. She reached out and touched the side of Dealer's seat. "Okay, so what have you decided to eat for dinner tonight?"

Lost in the unpleasant thought of driving her soon-to-be car to Catherine's house, Dealer forgot to answer.

"Dealer, quit fidgeting with the radio and … Oh, shit!" The scream split the air with instant fear as Dealer looked up and saw a truck parked in the middle of the street just around the bend of the road. The Volkswagen quickly approached it as panicked feet pumped the brakes. For a moment time stopped, and nothing happened. Then the Volkswagen slammed into the back of the semi-tractor trailer, careened into a guardrail, and sailed down the steep embankment. Dealer vaguely felt the car flipping over and over before it finally came to an abrupt stop. Her body was wedged between the seat and console, and she wasn't sure if anything was real.

In that brief moment of unreality she saw him. His look was contemplative, and then he smiled in a friendly way as if he was pleased about something. Then he laughed and sauntered away. Dealer's cries for help followed him.

"Mom, help me! Please, I'm stuck! Get me out of here!" The wind had been knocked out of her and she spoke with labored speech.

There was no response; only an eerie silence pervaded the forest around them, nothing but complete emptiness.

Blood dripped down the front of the leopard-covered seat, heavily splattering to the floor and onto Dealer's favorite white lace shirt.

"Mom? Are you okay? Mom?" Panic settled in.

Silence.

Dealer reached out to touch her mom, but there was so much blood. It was sticky and smelled of iron. Pulling back her hand in shock, Dealer looked down and realized it was her mom's blood. As black curtains faded her unreality, a hand held her down. The fuzzy face of the same man who had been standing by a nearby tree gazed at Dealer as if his mission was one of great importance. Then he started laughing as he whispered into her ear, "I'll be back, Dealer. You won't get away from me."

Chapter 2

A PALL SETTLED OVER the small farming community of Setauket, New York. One of its own had died. Wearing the black dress that her grandmother bought for her, Dealer numbly climbed into her dad's battered white Chevy pick-up. The day was cloudy and gloomy, one her mother would not have liked. They drove up the long drive to the Presbyterian church on the hill. It seemed as if the whole town had turned out to say good-bye to Nancy Townsend.

Dealer's friends sat in the crowded pews as she and her father made their way up to the front. Many of Nancy's friends were crying as Pastor Parkson talked about all her fine qualities. He even mentioned that she won a prize for her homemade peach jam at the county fair.

Dealer had no tears left to cry. It all seemed so surreal, and she could no longer feel grief and pain. Surely at any moment her mom would walk into the church, and the bad joke would end. But she didn't. The day was real.

Heavy footsteps left the church, and the procession moved to the cemetery. Dealer placed a white rose on her mom's coffin as it was being lowered into the ground. Her mind was incapable of registering so when she saw the same lady in black lace watching the funeral, she just stared. She was surreal, too. Nothing mattered anymore. Neighbors walked by the casket, silently mumbling a few words of prayer, then throwing a red rose into Mrs. Townsend's grave. Dealer heard the thump on the casket as each rose descended. The finality of it all hurt her ears. She turned away in sadness and joined her mom's parents. They were her new guardians for the summer while Dad sorted out his life. He had quickly taken up drinking and neglected to plant the spring crops.

Somebody decided Dealer would have stability if she lived with her grandparents. They would put her in counseling and give her a fresh life in the neighboring town away from her dad, the family farm, and all the tragedy until school began again in the fall.

The clouds were parting, and the hot sun peeked through. Dealer paused to look back. Her dad stood alone, watching the dirt scatter on the mahogany coffin, his shirt wet with perspiration. As if resigned to defeat, he held his hands in his pockets, and his chin rested on his chest.

It was then that she started to cry and could not stop. Grandfather put a comforting arm around her, but there were no words of comfort he could give. His heart was broken, too. He had just laid his own daughter to rest.

"Dad!" Dealer suddenly shouted. "Don't worry! I'll see you soon. You can visit me whenever you want. I'll be back before school begins."

He nodded his head, but the pools of emptiness in his eyes looked right through her. Desperate for a response, she pleaded once again. "Please don't worry about me! I'll be okay. I love you, Dad." He never said a word.

Her head hung down, Dealer silently walked toward her grandparents' car and away from what her life once was. The backseat greeted her with warm leather that did little to reassure her. She saw her dad, Robert Townsend III, still standing with the gravediggers as they continued to shovel dirt into the hole. Dealer put her hand on the glass in a silent wave of good-bye.

Chapter 3

IT WAS AWKWARD IN the beginning. Dealer's grandparents and dad hadn't really been close for a long time, and she didn't know what to say to them. They were strangers, and they didn't know what to say to her either. They had all lost someone special. While they seemed pleased that Dealer was living with them, they had to work to cope with the tragedy and with the presence of an angry teenager.

Thinking she would be at their home for quite a while, they had prepared Dealer's mom's old bedroom for her for what appeared to be a long stay. All around were Nancy's old things, reminders of the past — a dressing table with brushes and combs and pictures from her childhood.

One brush held a wisp of her mom's hair. Dealer gingerly touched the brush, caressing it and wishing her mom was standing beside her. Cheerleading pictures were on the vanity table alongside a picture of both parents at their high school prom. They looked so young and innocent, standing under a garland of flowers in their best clothes, smiling, holding hands.

Dealer's dad called once a week, but the conversations were stiff and formal. They talked, but so much was left unsaid. She missed him; she missed her family life. Maybe one day they could both get that feeling back. They never talked about her mom during the phone calls; they never talked about her at all. Dealer had a lot of unanswered questions so she tried to talk about the accident. Why had the semi-truck been parked in the middle of the highway just around the corner of the turn? Who was the man who had stood smiling on the embankment, who had touched her, who had spoken to her?

"Grandma," Dealer said one day after finally gathering the nerve to ask, "did the police ever find out who left the truck in the middle of the road?"

"Dealer, honey, they never found a truck. Your mom lost control of her car, hit the guardrail, and the two of you tumbled down the mountain and slammed into a tree. You went through so much in such a short period of time. You were in shock and must have imagined it. I'm sure it was very frightening." Sadness and empathy filled her reply.

"No, Grandma! There really was a parked truck. Are the police working on it? They never interviewed me. We have to find out who owns that truck!"

"Dealer, there was no truck. You hit the guardrail after your mom lost control of the car."

"No! That's not what happened!" was her adamant response.

"Okay, Dealer; let's talk about it later." The subject was closed as her Grandmother turned on the television.

Dealer knew that later was never going to come. She left her grandmother sitting on the sofa and went to her bedroom. The headphones blared Eminem in an attempt to block out the world and keep her from crying out in anger and frustration.

Dealer blamed herself for the accident. She had been in the front seat, texting her best friend Esther Reed and messing with the radio dial. She didn't want to believe that she had distracted her mom, causing her to lose focus and crash. What had caused the accident? She heard the phone ring.

"It's nice to hear from you. Yes, we're doing fine. Of course! Hold on a minute. I'll get her for you."

Intuitively Dealer must have known it was her dad calling. A little out of breath, she eagerly took the phone.

"Hey, Dealer; I really want you to come home. I miss you." He sounded happy again.

"I miss you, too, Dad. When can I come home?"

"School's about to start. I thought I'd drive over today. It's only a couple of hours' drive, and we can talk on our way back home. Would that be okay?"

"That would be perfect! I'll be ready when you get here."

Dealer shared the news with her grandparents. She couldn't believe how excited she was to go back home. Racing upstairs, she grabbed her suitcase and backpack. She was oblivious to the fact that she had two hours to pack. Haphazardly, she began stuffing her clothes and books into her bags. She stopped to admire a picture of her parents standing out in the cornfield on a cool, breezy day. Her mom's skirt whipped all around from the strong wind, and she seemed so young and shy. It wasn't hers to take, but Dealer picked it up anyway. Carefully she wrapped it in a tee shirt and placed it gently between her socks and underwear.

Her packing finished in less than ten minutes, Dealer tried to put her finger on the emotions she was feeling. The room that had been her sanctuary for the past few months now felt empty and lifeless. A part of her wanted to pick it up and take it with her, but other than some old keepsakes, there was nothing to replace the void her mom's death had created. Still, she felt a little guilty about leaving it.

The next hour and a half dragged on like an eternity. Dealer sat at the end of the sofa with her grandparents, nervously watching TV to pass the time. An uncomfortable silence settled in the air. For her grandparents, she was all that was left of their daughter — a stark reminder that Nancy was gone. They were both sad to see her leave and glad to have her go.

An incessant honking in the driveway meant Dad had arrived. Dealer hardly recognized him; he had lost a lot of weight, and the happiness she expected was gone. He looked so sad. She smiled tentatively at him. He tightened his grip on the sack of corn he was holding and awkwardly gave her a one-armed hug.

Dealer began to cry. It felt so right to be in her dad's arms after all that had happened, and yet they seemed so far apart.

"This has been the longest three months, Dealer. I can't believe how much you've grown; you look so much like your mom — same features, only shorter with laugh lines. When I look at you, I'm reminded of her and how much I miss her." A loud sigh escaped his lips.

"I'm sorry I haven't been here for you. You needed me, and I wasn't here. I needed to take care of some personal things, but that's done, and now I want you back home with me. It's not going to be easy without Mom, though. Life will be better if we're together."

Dealer felt a spasm of panic as she stared at him; he looked so lost. "The accident was my fault, Dad. I thought you didn't want me with you."

"Of course, not, Dealer! It wasn't your fault at all," he said with a hollow sadness. "Now get your stuff, and let's go home."

"Wouldn't you like something to eat before you take off?" Dealer's grandma questioned worriedly.

"How about if you make us a picnic basket of all the favorite things Dealer and I love to eat?"

She smiled a pleasing smile and headed to the kitchen to begin what turned out to be a feast of chicken, peanut butter and pineapple apricot jelly sandwiches, chips, oatmeal chip cookies, Cokes, and sweet iced tea all nestled in a beautiful wicker basket that held red and white checkered napkins and her best plastic silverware.

Grandpa walked over to his son-in-law and put his arm around his shoulder. "You don't look so good, son. Are you sure you can handle all of this?"

"No, I'm not sure, but I miss my little girl, and I know Nancy would want us to be together as a family."

"I understand. If you need us, we're only a phone call away. Do you need any money? I know times have been tough, and you didn't get the crops planted. Can we help in any way?"

Robert gave a slow smile. "Times have been tough, but I started working the land and got a part-time job at Walmart. I have a little money saved, and

I'm getting ready to plant corn for the spring. We'll be all right, but I know if I need you for anything, you'll be there for Dealer and for me."

Hidden in the shadows at the top of the staircase, Dealer listened as her dad and her grandpa exchanged small talk. Her belongings gathered, she suddenly needed to get out of the house. She ran down the stairs and almost collided with her grandma as she rounded the kitchen corner with the picnic basket. "Dealer, slow down!"

"Sorry, Grandma; I'm just excited!"

With a light swat in an effort to hold back her tears, she scolded, "Well, get going then. Your dad is waiting."

Her bright smile gave Dealer hope. "I love you so much!" Dealer hugged both of them with a sentiment that surprised her. "Thank you for having me. I hope I haven't been too much trouble."

"Well, not too much trouble," her grandfather said with a twinkle in his eye.

They said their good-byes, gave one more big hug and squeeze, then turned to leave. They had supported Dealer when she needed it most, and it hurt to leave them.

Suddenly a wisp of cold air sent shivers up her spine. The room felt somehow colder than it had been moments before. Dealer looked around as uneasiness settled in her consciousness, and she began to shake from the chill that swept through her as she picked up her stuff and walked out the door with her dad right behind her, carrying the picnic basket.

Dad opened the door of his 1982 Ford pick-up and shoved the picnic basket to the middle of the seat. He and Dealer climbed in and waved good-bye to her grandparents and blew kisses out the window toward them.

Chapter 4

AS THE SUN SANK toward the horizon, Battlefield Park along Lake George came into view. Situated just outside New York City, it boasted 28,160 acres that stretched north and west between the interstate and the highway. The area was steeped in American history. A crystal clear green lake lay just ahead, surrounded by acres of luscious thick grass. Dealer remembered her youth when she and her parents fished there, and whatever they caught they grilled on the barbecue that night.

The truck found its way onto a shaded spot beneath a sycamore tree. The air was brisk so Dealer grabbed her sweatshirt. They spread the feast Grandma had called a picnic onto a blanket they found behind the seat. For a moment the two sat in stiff silence and watched a young family playing on a nearby beach, the sound of their laughter bouncing off the sand.

Dealer reached in the picnic basket for a Coke and a peanut butter sandwich. Her dad leaned up against the old sycamore tree and sipped sweet iced tea. The scenery that surrounded them was calming, and Dealer's dad welcomed the opportunity to be nostalgic.

"Do you know how you got the nickname, Dealer?" An unusual softness soothed his words.

"If I do, I can't remember. How did I get it?"

He smiled, thinking back. "When you were little, I had a hard time paying for your medical bills and other things. Every Friday night your mom went out with her friends so I invited my friends to our farm for a friendly game or two of poker. One of those friends was your pediatrician, Dr. Tallmadge.

"I sat you at the table next to me, and you took on the job of replenishing the chips, salsa, and beer. Sometimes you dealt the cards. You loved it! As a matter of fact, you thrived within the circle of us grown men so the guys started calling you Dealer. Your mom was so mad when she found out, but the nickname stuck."

He paused for a second to reminisce, then he continued. "By the way, your doctor was not a very good card player and lost far more hands than he won so your check-ups were always free!"

"That's crazy, Dad! I love my nickname. I do vaguely remember dealing cards, but I didn't remember how I got my name. It's so much better than Evelyn."

"Your mom loved the name Evelyn; it was her favorite aunt's name," he managed while chewing, "but to me you've never quite felt like an Evelyn." Standing, he stretched, then picked up what was left of the food and put it back into the basket. "The sun's starting to set, and we've got at least an hour's drive left. Let's head home."

They decided to take the longer route back to the truck and walked away from the water and through the big tooth maple trees, wild mustard, and sturdy creosote bushes. It was a scene from nature the farm didn't have, and it felt good to stretch their legs.

There it was again. Dealer felt the hairs rise on the nape of her neck. She whipped around quickly, as if startled by something, but there was no one there. But there was someone there; she could feel it on the fringes of her awareness. She knew she was being watched.

Sliding into the front seat, Dealer pushed her uneasiness into a far corner of her mind. She chalked it up to being excited to go home, settle back in her own room, and wrap herself in the familiar daily routine of school, friends, and watching television.

But that didn't happen. It didn't happen because nothing was the same.

Chapter 5

HOME. THEY WERE FINALLY home. Dealer and her dad snuggled up on the couch to watch a zombie flick, but now that they were home, she felt like a brick wall had been built between them. He didn't respond to her glances or comments. Dealer imagined life would resume to its old habits, but it didn't. Nervously, she began rubbing the palms of her hands together as if wiping away the blood from her mom's body. It wasn't enough to relieve the stress so she followed her psychologist's orders and got up to stretch her legs and walk off the anxiety and tension she was feeling.

The movie was rather lame, and something else needed to fill her time. The hallway leading to the front door was dimly lit, and Dealer — lost in her thoughts — bumped into the doorknob on the attic door. The sensation of whacking her elbow's funny bone was not so funny, and she leaned up against the wall to rub it. The attic door stared back at her as if beckoning her up its stairs. Dealer realized she hadn't been in the attic since she was little and she and her mom put their creative minds together. Her mom had bought Mason jars from the Dollar Store and put feathers, seeds, buttons, and glitter in each one. They had made beautiful pictures on wooden canvases with those odds and ends. As a kid, Dealer remembered them being masterpieces. Her mom had said at least one of her creations belonged in a museum. She grinned, thinking about that moment.

Curiosity tugged to see if there was anything left of the pictures they had made together. The landing at the top of the attic stairs met Dealer with stale air and a sense of loneliness. The air was chilly, and the moon shone through the tall attic windows as if it were resting on the window sill. Dealer had little to fear of the dark creatures who haunted her nightmares, not here in this special place.

Empty bottles sat on a shelf, the resultant artwork probably long gone. Boxes and long-forgotten personal treasures littered the corners. Dealer ran her hand along the unpainted wood, dirt and dust collecting under her fingernails.

It was then she noticed a wallboard hanging loosely, rusted square-headed nails worming their way out of deteriorated holes. Peering through its crack was a glimpse of what appeared to be an old traveling trunk. I didn't know there was space behind this wall. Where did that trunk come from? Why is it there?

A hint of intrigue and euphoria ran through her veins as she attempted to pull the board away from the wall, but it was stuck. With surprising stealth Dealer quietly left the attic and retrieved a hammer and flashlight from her dad's red tool chest. Removing the board was a painstaking process; she could not risk drawing attention. Not yet. Age and dry rot were in her favor. Dealer finally managed to pull enough away to allow her to squeeze through the tight opening.

Flopping down on the dirty floorboards, she ran her hands along the antique's smooth, uneven edges. It was an old Revolutionary War trunk that bore a metal label with the year 1776 and Robert Townsend I inscribed on it. This trunk was way old; it had belonged to her great-great-grandfather. The magnitude of her discovery was almost unfathomable.

Overcome with elation as the discovery bubbled on the verge of hysteria, Dealer glanced around to make sure she was alone. Her find was worthy of Sherlock Holmes, and it had apparently been hidden in her family's farmhouse for centuries.

Brushing away the dirt and grime that covered the chest, she realized that it was locked. For a moment, discouragement settled in — but just for a moment. Her eyes scoured the fairly large space for some type of tool to open it. Dusty, faded orange-colored draperies as thin as paper allowed light to filter in where a once-used roll-top desk stood. It was littered with pieces of fabric and paints, colored pencils with leads worn down to nothing, an old pin cushion, its sawdust insides spilling out its seams — and an old metal letter opener. It was Dealer's best bet for breaking open that lock.

Determination wasn't enough. She knew nothing about locksmithing, and the lock was stiff and slightly oxidized. Decoding the levers with a letter opener would be impossible. She gave up and sat back on her legs to think of another solution. The trunk was a family heirloom so taking a hammer to the lock was not an option.

Slowly Dealer worked to unfold her tingling legs. There had to have been a key. Where was it? She went back to her mom's desk and sifted through the debris. The feel of the dust made her skin crawl with frustration. She couldn't find a key. All manner of trinkets, pieces of wood, bits of candles, and colorless ribbons were strewn in the drawers. The bookshelf held even more unorganized junk.

There were old papers and books piled in confusion. Moving aside a book on photography, Dealer had a thought. Her mom always kept special things — Grandmother's cameo, her first baby tooth, Dad's college graduation ring — in her glass button jar. But where was it? It had been years since she'd seen it.

Then she remembered. Her mom kept it in a plastic storage bucket along with squares of material to make a quilt. But where was the bucket? She used the flashlight to scan the base of the walls. Old pictures and a rack of clothes were in a corner by the chimney. She shifted the clothes to look behind them, accumulated dust choking her. Sure enough, there it was. Giddy feelings tumbled in her stomach as she dragged the bucket out from under the rack. She tugged at the lid until it popped open. There nestled between the folds of fabric was the button jar, its metal lid speckled with rust. Dealer removed the lid, and there it was, a shiny, oddly-shaped key.

"Dealer, where are you?" Finally Dad had realized she was no longer watching the movie and had disappeared.

"I'm in the attic!"

Dealer could feel his tiredness as he climbed the steps, but she was glad for his company.

"Hey there. What'd you find up here? Some ghosts?" Then he caught himself.

"No ghosts but look over in the corner, behind the wall. I found an old trunk." The corners of Dealer's mouth were twitching with adrenalin.

"Looks like you did some damage pulling away that piece of wood in the walls, young lady." Her dad's voice frowned with disapproval.

Dealer's fingers tightened on the small key she held in her hand. Then she made a decision. She relaxed her grasp and shoved her open palm in front of her dad. Moments before the key felt light as a feather; now it was heavy like lead.

"Mmm. Looks like you've found yourself an adventure. Where did you find this?"

"I found the key in Mom's old button jar."

"Well, let's see if it works." Dealer's dad dropped to his hands and knees and squeezed through the tight opening of the wall. "Hand me the flashlight, Dealer."

She almost couldn't contain her excitement; maybe there was a treasure. God knew they needed the money, at least that's what Grandpa had said. Dealer knew her dad had lied; he wasn't planting anything. There wasn't any money to plant corn. She pushed the thought aside and carefully slid inside the crawl space next to her father.

He took a deep breath in an attempt to stop his quivering hands so he could get the key in the lock. He was sweating and looked over at Dealer. She responded with an anxious look of her own. She knew he didn't want her to know he had been drinking again. He claimed to have been sober for two weeks. He had been dealt a lousy hand, and Mom's death had sent him spiraling out of control. He was trying to take steps to get that control back.

It was a tough break. In an irrational moment he had taken out a short-term loan using the farm as collateral. Walmart didn't pay much so the loan went unpaid, and the bank manager, Mr. Simcoe, had begun the foreclosure process. Maybe just this once Dad would catch a break, and something in this trunk would be of enough value to get them out of hot water.

Surprisingly, the key turned easily in the keyhole, the mechanism releasing its long-held grasp. Dad began to slowly lift the lid. It groaned and squealed from lack of use. The hinges caught, and it took a strong shove to break their reluctance. Clouds of dust gathered in the air when the lid hit the floor. Inside were papers, nothing but papers. Robert Townsend III noticed only letters. He saw nothing of value — no gold, no silver, nothing worth having or so he thought. He inched back out of the crawl space without saying a word, disappointment wracking his soul.

"Where are you going, Dad?"

"It's your find, honey. Perhaps it's time to go to bed, and tomorrow you can spend some time and look through the letters. Maybe there's some history there."

"I'm not tired. And besides, how can I possibly sleep, knowing the thoughts of my ancestors are just waiting to be revealed? They were important to Mom so they're important to me."

"Of course, they are. I'll leave you to your adventures but don't stay up too late. I have a long day ahead of me tomorrow so I'm tucking in. Crops have to be planted before it's too late." He did his best to put heart in his words, but his delivery was filled with discouragement.

Dealer felt badly for her dad and had no idea what to say to bring him out of his melancholy. So she let it go, including his lie of planting a crop.

Dealer eased herself to the floor next to the trunk and crossed her legs. As she rummaged carefully through the trunk's belongings, she realized that the contents reminded her of an old cedar chest rather than a traveling trunk. There were papers, letters, and envelopes of different sizes, each one dingy and marked by time; a ragged piece of stained lace that may have been part of a baby's bonnet; an old Valentine addressed to a cherished lover; what was left of a dried bouquet of meadow flowers, their colors lost to the years with only an imagination to bring them back.

She decided to inspect one object at a time. Picking up a bulging envelope, she gently slid out a single sheet of handwritten paper and an object about the size of a chicken egg. A small gasp escaped her lip as she fell back against the broken wood.

Trying to read the paper was impossible; it was clearly written in code, a code that she had seen displayed in the Setauket library when studying its history just last year. Her memory served her well. She recalled that all sorts of methods of coding were used during the American Revolution to further a cause or its agenda. During that time an innkeeper named Anna Strong, who was part of George Washington's spy ring, hung her black underwear on the clothesline with handkerchiefs to tell Caleb Brewster which inlet other spies would gather at and where the British would be landing. She also remembered that Washington had used the very code she held in her hands to pass information to his spies.

Washington's chief spymaster, Major Tallmadge, created a system that substituted digits for words. Having seen a picture of the code at the library, Dealer remembered that 728 was code for Long Island, 77 was code for firearms, and 88 was code for city. There was also a number for each month. Tallmadge made four copies of the code: one for himself, one for Brewster, one for Dealer's ancestor Robert Townsend, and one for General Washington.

She put the envelope and its contents to the side. Peering inside the trunk again, she noticed a shiny object and realized it was a stone set within ornate prongs on the back of an oval locket held by a simple yet elegant chain, each link double twisted to its partner.

She cradled the polished chunk of amber in her palm as if it were the most precious object in the world. Under the dull bulb of the flashlight, it looked little more than a shiny brown rock, but it felt warm to the touch. Light reflected off its surface, and in the very center, tiny letters hung motionless, preserved across hundreds of years, a moment frozen forever in amber. I wonder who this belonged to.

May our love last a lifetime.
355

Dealer turned the mounted stone over so she could inspect the locket. Delicate scrolls were etched in minute detail on its surface.

She noticed a tiny catch on its side and gently pressed it. Dust, dirt, and time had settled in, and it refused to open. Suddenly Dealer was overcome with an overwhelming curiosity to see what was inside so she pressed harder. The locket sprang open immediately.

It held the images of a man and a woman, both smiling with wise eyes at the photographer. Dealer admired their expressions very much. She had no idea who the beautiful woman was but she looked familiar, and she was quite certain the man was a relative because he looked just like her father.

She felt she was getting a glimpse of history from Robert Townsend in the form of a lucky charm, or possibly it was a gift to him or a gift from him to a lover.

"Maybe one of the female spies," she said excitedly to no one but the dust mites and herself. Why the thought of spies and lovers crossed her mind was beyond her, but it did.

The flashlight dimmed considerably, its battery running low, and Dealer knew the moment would have to wait until tomorrow. She carefully tucked the letters neatly back inside the old trunk and closed the lid. Then she locked it. Placing the key on the amber necklace, she slipped the chain gently over her head and around her neck. Maybe this had all once belonged to Robert Townsend. Her dad was right. Dealer had stumbled upon an adventure after all.

Chapter 6

DISAPPOINTED THAT SHE DIDN'T have time to read the letters, Dealer decided to do some computer research. She walked down the attic stairs, the warmth of the rock necklace against her chest somehow comforting. The bedroom she and her mother had decorated together — yellow curtains and a matching yellow polka-dot comforter — was her haven of solace. Munchies close by, she sat down and began to research anything that referred to a code used in the American Revolutionary War.

In the Spy Master Code she saw an old copy of one code that was reproduced, but it was too difficult to read. She found interesting information in George Washington's Spymaster regarding spy activities conducted under Washington's guidance during the Revolution. It also offered an overview of the espionage activities during the war throughout the country and even in the town of Setauket. Dealer found it hard to imagine the stately George Washington involved in spy activities. It seemed so dangerous and clandestine.

There was much to learn so she decided a trip to the Emma S. Clark Library on the Village Green after school was needed. To be able to touch the books and turn their pages would yield far more than scrolling on her computer screen. Hours later, she narrowed her search and made notes of the code that Benjamin Tallmadge had written for Washington. That tucked neatly in the back pocket of her jeans, she set the alarm for six a.m. and climbed into bed. Excitement masked her fatigue as thoughts, curiosities, questions, and the thrill of attending her first day back to school bombarded her consciousness. Sleep evaded her.

- - - - - - - - - - - - - - -

The call to get up after a restless night came early. The shower did little to jump-start Dealer, but when she put on the new clothes her grandmother had bought her — blue jeans, a yellow shirt, and tennis shoes, a sense of confidence woke her up. She had not realized it before, but yellow was definitely her favorite color. It showcased her emerald green eyes and long black lashes.

She skipped stairs until she almost tripped and decided it was better to walk into the kitchen to get her lunch. Dad was asleep on the couch; this was not a good sign. Dealer prayed he hadn't been drinking again because that would land her right back with her grandparents. She wasn't supposed to know about his drinking problem, but she did. The many bottles of cheap wine that filled the recycle bin were unmistakable. It broke her heart that there was nothing she could do about it.

Picking up her backpack from where she had piled it, Dealer reread the note that had been left for her: "Have a great day! See you tonight! Love, Dad." As she turned to walk out the door, a flurry of movement caught her eye. Someone was moving swiftly across the hallway and up the stairs toward the attic. A bit of fear gripped her gut as she hugged the door jamb and peered around the corner. Now there was nothing there. It seemed uncanny, but in retrospect Dealer thought the someone was wearing an elegant long black dress with a delicate lace shawl and a black bonnet on her head. Should she be afraid? She was afraid! Her sense of anxiety just wouldn't go away.

It was time for the school bus. If she hurried, it would not leave without her. She didn't want to miss it. Today was to be a new experience. Last year she attended Ward Melville Middle School. That seemed like a lifetime ago. Now she was a freshman at Ward Melville High School.

As excited as she was, Dealer found room to worry about making new friends, figuring out where classes were, and adjusting to high school life.

This wasn't a new concept, but it was a new experience for her. She ran to the bus stop.

- - - - - - - - - - - - - -

Entering the high school cautiously, Dealer zigged and zagged down the corridor, dodging all the hurrying students and frantically searching for her homeroom, which was also her English class. Then she heard it — the late bell. She hated the sound of that bell because she hated to be late. Her breath came in tiny gasps as her throat tightened. "Stop it," she chided herself. "Now is not the time to have a panic attack, not on the first day!" She had enough problems.

Forcing herself to slow down and breathe deeply, Dealer's nerves began to calm. Deep breath; count to ten. The grief counselor's voice was in her head.

Were high school teachers as nice as middle school teachers? Probably not. Her nervousness about being late increased.

Finally Dealer found the door she was looking for — D-12. It was closed, of course. Sweaty palms tentatively opened it. She slipped in. The room was only partially full. Relief almost overwhelmed her as she realized others had to be late, too.

"Take a seat, Evelyn," the teacher growled. "We'll see how long it takes everyone else to show up. Then we'll get started."

How did she know my name? Hers was written in pink neon on a dry erase board — Ms. Arnold. The amber stone around Dealer's neck began to burn. Something was wrong. She not only felt it, she sensed it as well. Unconsciously she began rubbing the palms of her hands together. Deep breath; count to ten.

The teacher impatiently waved her hand in the general direction of an empty seat amongst the sea of anxious faces that stared back at Dealer. Ms. Arnold walked over to a disorganized bookcase and removed a burgundy notebook. Another classmate entered the classroom and took his share of grief from her. Another one followed after him; Ms. Arnold called him Dexter. It was going to be a long 50 minutes.

Thankfully Ms. Arnold ignored the tardy students for the rest of the class period. Dealer paid little attention to anything that was said; instead she took in her surroundings. The walls were a cold steel gray, almost identical to the color of Ms. Arnold's eyes. Three small posters littered the space directly opposite where she sat, the print too small to read and obviously created before the advent of the wheel. The floor was scuffed, and many of the desks had chips and dents. Overall the room felt as old as Ms. Arnold looked — about fifty, but then every teacher looked about fifty to Dealer. She was definitely older than her thirty-six-year-old dad.

The bell suddenly rang, and panic set in. Dealer tapped the tardy boy on the shoulder. "Could you show me the way to my next class? I have no sense of direction, and I'm completely lost."

Looking down at the map she held in her hand, he said, "Sure. It's right across the hall from where I'm going." Dealer nodded her appreciation and shuffled to the door, following him like a lost dog down a quiet hall that seemed to dead end, but it eventually opened to a staircase. "These stairs go to the basement, but now it's barricaded with locks and a fence," he explained. They walked down another flight of stairs. A large black "P" painted on a red door just past a locked gate on the landing below came into view.

"Why is the stairway going down from here gated and padlocked?"

"Because nobody's supposed to go down there, that's why." It was as if he thought the question had been a stupid one.

"Did you ever go down there?"

"Why would I? There's nothing down there. You ask a lot of questions, uh, ... What's your name anyway?" His lopsided grin showed genuine interest.

"My name's Evelyn, but please call me Dealer."

"All right, Dealer, as long as you call me Dex," he countered.

Dealer smiled at him. It fit that he didn't want to be called Dexter. Not ready to let the matter go, she gently elbowed him. "I bet you have gone down there."

"Maybe I have; maybe I haven't. Maybe someday I'll tell you more about what's down there, but right now we've got to get to class." He motioned toward the green swinging doors to the left, pushed them open, and directed her to her history class.

"Wait, you have to help me with this map," she pleaded. "I don't understand any of it."

Her pleading touched a soft spot. "Next period is lunch so I'll meet you right outside those brown doors." He pointed to the other end of the hallway. "You'll find me near an old maple tree. There are benches so we can sit and eat and talk."

"Great!" Dealer said as she stepped into her next challenge. Was she relieved? Oh, yeah!

Chapter 7

WALKING OUT OF HISTORY class Dealer had the thought that as a teacher Ms. Grace Rachel Martin wasn't so bad. It was the first day of school, and she played a game with the class to get to know her students. Students wrote their names on a 3"x5" card and one interesting fact about themselves. The next day she would see if she remembered the particulars. Then she was going to give the class a mental challenge to see if anyone could get the answer. The winner of each day's game would win a prize. As a teacher, she was definitely a novel idea.

Dealer walked down the hall and out the brown doors. Maybe having lunch with Dex would really make the day turn out to be okay. She spotted him sitting under the maple tree just like he said. Riley Strong and Aiden Brewster, homeroom classmates, joined him. Aiden was an athletic-looking boy who wore glasses. Riley was willowy, long golden blonde hair falling to her collar bone and framing a perfect complexion. She was someone Dealer could certainly be envious of.

Secretly Dealer had hoped it would be just Dex and her eating lunch together, but that was a selfish thought. She needed to make some new friends so sharing his time with others should be a good thing. She noticed some middle school friends, but they never looked her in the eye, nor had they ever contacted her after her mom had died. They probably hadn't known what to say.

"Mr. Simcoe is foreclosing on our house, too," Dealer heard Riley state matter-of-factly as she approached the group.

Did I hear her right? she wondered. *Did Riley just say that her family was in the same mess her family was in?*

Dex looked up to see Dealer, and she turned her head slightly in embarrassment. She was about to be a fifth wheel. Everyone went silent.

"Hi, Dealer! Have you met Riley and Aiden? They're in Ms. Arnold's class with us."

"Hello! How did you like her grilling and drilling of everyone?" Aiden wasn't one to be shy.

"As well as can be expected I guess," Dealer commented. "Does she get any better?"

"Nope. What you see is what you get, and it isn't pretty." On top of being pretty, Riley wasn't shy either. The three settled in like an old pair of tennis shoes.

"Great …" Dealer half moaned.

"I told Dealer I would help her learn the layout of the new wing to the school. You guys can add anything if I miss something so she doesn't keep getting lost."

"It's really easy once you get the hang of it," Aiden said, grabbing the map and taking charge of the task of educating Dealer. "Think of the spokes of a wheel with each corridor running off the center and then at the end intersecting a circular corridor that joins them all."

Dex made sure he added his two cents' worth. "Don't forget there are six buildings with six corridors in all — A through F — and they're all color coded."

"See here." Riley stabbed a manicured nail at the piece of paper. "This is A so the doors are red — red like an apple. B is blue. C is yellow like corn."

"Really? C is for corn?" Dealer found she couldn't help herself and began to laugh.

"Yes, C is for corn! Do you have a better analogy? D is for dirt because the doors are brown."

Everyone chuckled except Dealer. "You have got to be kidding me! Letters and colors and spokes!"

Dex began to rub his temples. "Oh, my …"

"No kidding here. This is for real." Riley grinned. "We just made all that up!"

"I've been to Paris, and their airport terminal is similar to this," Aiden insisted.

"It looks like Setauket has the French to thank," Dealer whispered. "Look,

Dex, how am I supposed to do this? I have to learn this entire map in one day! There's no way I'm going to find all of my classes before the late bell rings!"

"Relax, Dealer. Forget about the colors for now. Here's your science class — Building C, Room 212. Look at the end of the hall. See the big C? My class is right down the hall. I'll meet you outside after class and show you around some more so just wait for me."

Before she knew it, her three new friends were on their feet and hurrying away, each promising to meet up after school. All too quickly they were gone, swallowed up in a mass of sweaty teenagers who merged as one down the hall in a slowly moving wave of tee shirts, short skirts, and jeans that fell down below butt cheeks.

Chapter 8

CLASSES WERE FINALLY OVER for the day. Dealer raced out the door, bumping others who clearly wanted out as badly as she did. There was no sign of Dex, and uneasiness set in. The outside air was stifling even though it wasn't so hot. Then she saw him off in the distance. He was talking to some kids by the statue of George Washington, his friends Aiden and Riley in tow. Dealer stopped just before she reached them to read what was written on the gold plate on the platform:

> *In recognition to the Culper Spy Ring and*
> *the brave people of Setauket*
> *that fought the British on these hallowed grounds.*
> *America will be forever in your debt.*

Dealer had never read much about the Culper Spy Ring, but she suddenly remembered her find in the attic and wondered if it had anything to do with these people.

"Interesting, isn't it?" Riley drawled as she walked over to where Dealer stood.

"Yeah, it is. I'm curious about the Culper Spy Ring. They were an important part of the American Revolution's history. I'm even more intrigued since the discovery I made in our attic..."

Dex overheard her comments. "You found something interesting in your attic? Was it a treasure map? Will it lead to gold?" Dealer knew he wasn't trying to poke fun at her, but she took offense to it just the same.

"Go ahead and laugh if you want."

"Sorry, Dealer. All kinds of stories have floated around this town for years — so many it's become a joke. What did you find?"

Forgetting Dex was going to give her a further lesson on the school's floor plan, Dealer became wrapped up in sharing her find.

"I was going through some of my mother's things and found an antique trunk full of letters written in some type of code. I have no idea how to decipher them so I'm going to the library to see what I can uncover about George Washington and his secret spy ring during the Revolutionary War. Seeing his statue just reminded me."

"Heck, this town is full of Revolutionary War descendants, including us, so we'll all go with you if you like! Do you have the letters with you?" Dex probed, his curiosity clearly at a high level.

"No, I left the letters at home, but I did copy part of one and some other information I uncovered. I suppose four heads are better than one. It will be interesting to find out more about the Culper Spy Ring."

Aiden was all in. "Definitely! And who knows? Maybe we can use some of the information we dig up to help us write a paper for history class. You know we're going to have to write at least one!"

At three-thirty the researchers raced to the Emma Clark library. Riley took the lead. She set her books down on the library table next to the framed portrait of George Washington and his secret code and studied it for a moment. It looked complicated, yet somehow it had worked. She snapped a quick picture. Aiden and Dealer joined her.

"The code looks like it's a combination of words and numbers, and the other secret writing hanging next to Tallmadge's pictures is the part of the cipher with all of the names of important people in the Culper Ring. They were all assigned a number for covert identification," informed Dex.

Dealer knew this, but of course, her emotions let him take the lead. Dex was cute, with his sandy blond hair, tan face, big light blue eyes, and incredible body. What female in her right mind wouldn't let him take the lead?

"The British spy John Andre even had his own cipher, and he used a rare invisible ink. He wrote a letter to Benedict Arnold's wife Peggy, and it included the letter A, which meant acid had to be used to decipher the code." Riley was summarizing what she had read in a biography about Benedict Arnold.

"I wonder how many ciphers were out there and if we will ever be able to find all of the codes written to decipher the letters I have at home?" Dealer half-mindedly said to herself.

"Are there lots of letters?" Curiosity and intrigue filled Riley's voice as she wriggled between Dealer and the chair next to her.

"Oh, yeah, quite a few." Dealer's response was a dull one.

"You sound a little discouraged. Right now we have nothing, but it's worth a try, and maybe if we're real lucky, we'll find a treasure. I mean, in all the stories I've read, if there is an old trunk, there's got to be a treasure map, right? Maybe we can save our town and be heroes!" Aiden had an answer for everything.

"You watch too many movies, dude," Dex scoffed.

"Let's take pictures of each of the ciphers," Riley suggested. "Then, if it's okay with you, Dealer, we'll all go to your house and work on decoding a letter or two. You never know! There may be treasure!"

The amber gemstone necklace warmed on Dealer's chest. She thought it was strange but ignored the sensation until she looked down an aisle of books and saw the beautiful lady. She was wearing the same black lace shawl she had been wearing yesterday. She glided past, and Dealer smelled her lavender perfume.

Dealer turned away and lifted the locket from her chest. As soon as she opened it, she knew the lady she had just seen was the same one who held the space next to the handsome man. Who are you? Why are you here?

Dealer knew no one else had seen her so she kept quiet. Her new friends would surely think she was crazy. For all she knew she was crazy.

"Sounds like a great plan." Dealer stood up and looked out the library window. "Do you see that guy over there behind the sycamore tree? Who is he?"

"That's my new friend, the foreclosure guy, Simcoe," answered Aiden sarcastically. "And he's not a nice guy."

"What's he doing here?" Dex asked disgustedly. "I already bumped into him once earlier today."

"Do you think he's following us?" Worry filled Dealer's voice. "I'm scared he's going to foreclose on our farm."

"You, too? We're all being foreclosed on by that guy; he is evil incarnate." Aiden made sure he said the last part of his sentence loud enough for everyone in the library to hear.

"I can't believe how white he is. He looks like a stigoli," Riley added with a shudder.

"He looks like a what?"

"It's a Romanian vampire," Riley replied.

"Now that's just plain weird, even for you." Dex had been quiet throughout the exchange.

"And it's such a big word, Riley! Where did you hear that from?" Aiden really couldn't help himself.

"Ah, it was in a movie I saw once."

"You're just showing off."

"I'm not, but just the same, that guy gives me the creeps."

For a few moments, they stood and chatted, somehow reluctant to move. Time and space seemed to hold them in place. "We're burning daylight, folks," Dex finally prodded. "What are we waiting for?"

"Food! Am I the only one who is hungry?" Aiden groaned. "Maybe we can stop and pick up some on our way to Dealer's house. Anything's fine; I just need some food!"

"Sure! I'm hungry!" Dex chimed in. "A Subway sandwich will tide us over before dinner."

Dealer opened the big oak library door for everyone and walked right into Mr. Simcoe. "Excuse me, sorry," she stuttered. Immediately her chest became hot from the pulsating rock.

"You should be! Watch how fast you open that door, young lady!" Mr. Simcoe looked down at her with an uncomfortable sternness. "Wait! Aren't you the drunk's daughter?"

Dealer felt herself turning a deep red, and tears started rolling down her face.

"I was just kidding; you're the Townsend girl, aren't you?" Simcoe back-pedaled.

"You bastard," Dex mumbled under his breath, but Dealer was already halfway out of sight. She brushed past him and ran home, never looking back.

To her surprise, her friends followed her. She ran up the stairs and onto the porch. Dex quickly held the front door open for her. It took everything she had to maintain her composure.

"You don't need to be embarrassed, Dealer," he said. We all have our own bags to carry, but Simcoe's a shit for saying that."

Dealer shrugged her shoulders, pushed him aside, and went into the house. The uncomfortable subject was dropped as the rest of her friends came through the door. The kitchen table seemed to be the place to land. Dealer liked having her friends over; it meant any confrontation with her dad would at least be momentarily avoided. Backpacks piled on the floor, and the thud of kitchen chairs set the group in motion.

"I think we forgot about food," Aiden made a point to remind everyone. "Let's order a large pizza, and I'll buy. I'm that starved!" His idea was met without whines or complaints, and 20 minutes later they forgot every manner they had been taught and dived in.

"I'll have your crust, Dealer," Aiden said as he grabbed the browned dough she had thrown in the box lid. "Waste is a terrible thing!"

"Yep, it is, but the crust?! Be my guest!" Dealer giggled.

Clearly Riley was preoccupied. She spoke little, ate her pizza, and knitted her brow as she wrote scribbles on her napkin. She was the first to make sense of Dealer's notes. "Look! I've decoded the letter using the two papers we photographed at the library! Check it out."

They began to read the cipher. (Using the code found in the back of this book, see if you can decipher the message.)

723

640 727 50 722 55 703

723 688

120 374 ouu

355

"I wonder if the gold was ever found?" Dealer pondered out loud. Her chest began to heat up from the amber. Was the Lady in Black Lace trying to tell her something? She didn't normally believe in ghosts, but she was beginning to. Beads of sweat formed above her upper lip; she hoped no one noticed.

Dex didn't think so. "I think we would have heard or read about it if it was found. It would be a rush, though, to find some old letters, maps, and codes that we can study so we can learn more about the Culper Ring and the missing gold — if it is still missing."

"Okay, Dealer. You're the one with the trunk and the only one of us with anything so far," Aiden said. "We'll follow your lead."

Digressing from the topic at hand, Riley asked Dealer, "So your farm is being foreclosed on like the rest of ours?"

"Oh, my God, it's very close to being foreclosed on. It's awful!"

"It's awful for all of us. Like most every other family in the community, Mr. Simcoe gave my parents a loan with a variable interest rate attached. The economy tanked, and now they can't make the higher payments. My mom shed a lot of tears over it. She mentioned something about a balloon payment, but I don't know what that means," Dex said sadly.

"It means we're all going to lose our homes; that's what it means," Aiden said matter-of-factly.

"Does anyone know what a balloon payment is?"

"I'm not sure," Dealer mumbled. "I think Dad told me it has something to do with interest and a large sum of money being owed at the end of a certain time period on a loan. Most people who sign up for that kind of financing end up losing their homes."

Dealer wasn't interested in talking about bankers and loans. "Hey, enough of the bad stuff. How about we all go up to the attic before it gets dark?"

"That all sounds great, but I can't get Mr. Simcoe out of my head. I think he has ulterior motives," Riley said as she folded her napkin and then reopened it.

"What do you mean by ulterior motives, Riley?" asked Aiden.

"Well, he could be looking for the treasure just like we are, and he doesn't know where it is so he's following us and baiting us."

"You think so? That seems like a stretch but maybe." Aiden wasn't convinced.

"I'm certainly going to look into it. I'm going back to the library to check through the newspaper archives. I should be able to find out how many homes are being foreclosed on. It has to be public record. While I'm at it, I'll take some time and research some Setauket history. In the meantime, maybe the rest of you can find out something about that missing shipment of gold."

"Or a treasure map!" Aiden added emphatically.

"I agree with Riley. I think Simcoe is up to no good. You go to the library if you want. I'm going to take another look at some of those letters in my mom's trunk. Maybe I can decipher enough to help us find a lost shipment of British gold."

"Don't think you get to have all that fun by yourself! I didn't come all this way for nothing!" Aiden picked up the trash and threw it in the garbage can. "We're coming up with you!"

"You've got that right," Dex agreed. "Either somebody found it and said nothing, or it's just waiting to be discovered. My nose is itching. Let's go check out that trunk."

Chapter 9

RILEY LICKED HER FINGERS in satisfaction and sprang off her chair. "See you guys later." She nudged her chair under the table.

Hurrying back to the library, past the sub shop and the town center, she moved right through the library door and began picking up newspapers, books, and maps she had seen earlier. It seemed like only a moment ago since she had left Dealer's house. Her excitement drove her at a pace that even surprised her.

"What are you doing, Riley?" Ms. Arnold hissed. Riley dropped the papers she had been holding, her body jerking in response. *What a witch! She nearly scared me to death!*

"I'm looking through newspapers and books to help me with an assignment."

Ms. Arnold continued her icy glare. "Make sure you put them back when you're finished."

Riley calmed herself as she picked up the scattered newspapers. *What is she doing here at this hour of the day?* From now on we need to be more discreet. Something was wrong. There was something eerily odd about Ms. Arnold and about Mr. Simcoe, too, for that matter. Both of them gave her the creeps.

- - - - - - - - - - - - - - -

The rest of the group trudged up the staircase to the attic. With care, Dealer lifted a handful of the letters out of the trunk and began to sort them, handing a pile to Aiden and a pile to Dex. A bunch more were still at the bottom of the trunk. Dealer seriously doubted if they could finish deciphering even one letter. Each of them set out to look for something of meaning or importance. They knew it sounded like a fantasy, but that was the hope the four of them clung to.

Dealer's dad didn't seem to be getting any closer to saving the farm from foreclosure. He was attempting to find a bank that would refinance it, but she wasn't sure what that meant. She just wanted to continue to live in the home where her mom's presence permeated every corner. Nothing else was acceptable.

The rest of the afternoon was dedicated to the attic and arranging the letters according to ciphers, maps, and miscellaneous other things. It was very hot, and the orange drapes provided no protection from the sweltering sun pouring through them. Bodies glistened with sweat, but it took the sun's salute as it fell below the horizon to drive the friends back to the kitchen table and better light.

Painstakingly the letters were again divided into two piles, those that needed reading and those that needed deciphering. One of the letters was written to Dealer's great-great-grandfather by a lady known only as agent 355. Dealer found she couldn't read it aloud. It was heartbreaking; they had loved each other.

"Agent 355 was living in her family's home on Second Street. Because of the Garrison Act that allowed the British to live in homes of Americans, John Andre, an officer in Howe's army, ordered the Darragh family out of their residence so he could hold officer meetings.

"The lady of the house protested. In her possession was a letter from her brother, who was an Irish officer in the British military. The letter stated that she came from an aristocratic family. She took it to General Howe to use as leverage in her complaint about the treatment of a loyal family. Out of sympathy for such an important family, Howe gave in to her protestations and agreed that his soldiers would not live there. However, he insisted that occasionally his men be allowed to use the large parlor for meetings.

"This particular lady was a patriot for America after she witnessed her mother being thrown into a fire by the Redcoats and risked her life to listen in on John Andre's secret meetings while hiding in a nearby closet. She lived in constant fear that she might be discovered and would, therefore, be hanged. She was a Quaker, a religious sect that did not believe in war, but she felt she must help Washington by any means to save her new country, particularly since the British had taken over the homes of her friends and terrorized good people from her church."

"Wow! How do you know all of this stuff?" Dex was amazed.

"In part from some history I've learned, and I've been reading the letters that didn't need deciphering. This one is a poem written by Shakespeare with clues hidden between the lines."

Your hand lie open in the long fresh grass-
The finger points look through rosy bloom:
Your eyes smile peace. The pasture gleams and glooms
'Neath billowing skies that scatter and amass.
All around our nest, far as the eye can pass,
Are lemon Kingcup-fields with silver edge
Where the cow parsley skirts the hawthorn-hedge.
'Tis visible silence, still as the hour-glass.
Deep in the sun-searched growths the dragonfly
Hangs like a blue thread loosened from the sky
So this winged hour is dropped to us from above.
Oh! Clasp we to our hearts, for deathless dower,
This close-companioned inarticulate hour
When twofold silence was the song of love.

"Okay, what's that supposed to mean?" Aiden shrugged his shoulders in confusion.

"Remember what the General Spies book at the library said? Some of the information was written in invisible ink. Look at the space between the sonnets; we need to decipher what's written there. Invisible ink can be made visible if we're determined and careful. It's a time-consuming process, and right now we don't have time to put hours of effort into every single piece of paper. See the rough scratches that were probably made from a feather pen and inkwell? Let's look at this paper under the bright stove light. Dex, grab the magnifying glass in the top left kitchen drawer. Maybe we can see if there are any clues," Dealer rambled on, flinching when the rock on her chest suddenly grew very warm.

"Why is this word *lemon* out of context in the letter?" Aiden wondered.

"Well, it could be to alert someone that they must use a lemon in some way, which is acidic in nature, to expose the hidden message," Dex observed.

"Before we do anything, why don't you Google it, Aiden? To make sure that lemon is a clue and can be used on an old document."

"You're right, Dealer." He picked up his phone and began his search on invisible ink and old documents. After a few scrolls and grunts, he said, "Here it says that lemon was used to bring up hidden messages. I think it's safe to try."

"Maybe it will come through, but we have to be careful so we don't ruin the whole thing. We'll treat it like a stained piece of laundry — test a small area first." Dealer felt extremely nervous. The last thing she wanted to do was destroy the letter, but the promise of gaining a valuable clue overrode her fear.

Her hands shook as Dex took the fragile paper from her and placed it on a cookie sheet sitting on the counter. The two stood around him as he exercised a deliberate tenseness to applying little bits of lemon juice. Sweat began to form on the sides of his face.

"I see some lettering coming through! Quick! Put on a little more!" Dealer urged.

Slowly letters began to emerge. There was the message that had been waiting to be discovered.

"What's it say?" Aiden asked excitedly.

Dealer leaned over the document and quickly began to decipher it. Looking over her shoulder, Dex immediately saw that the letter was from Lydia Darragh, and it was addressed to Culper, Jr.

On a tiny island, only as big as your hand, resting in Lake George in the mountainous area of northeastern New York holds a treasure dating back to the French and Indian Wars.

John Andre had a meeting in our parlor discussing the whereabouts of a treasure that was left in haste during the French and Indian War, and he was sending a party of soldiers to retrieve it. If we could get to it first, my love, it is possible we could help to save our men from the cold and hunger. I digress; let me continue. George James Abercrombie's combined British and Colonial Forces had portaged a fleet of small boats from the upper Hudson River over land to Lake George during the summer of 1759. Their objective was to attack the French bastion at Fort Carillon at the southern tip of Lake Champlain. This fort is now called Fort Ticonderoga. Abercrombie commanded over twelve thousand troops aboard almost nine hundred boats. At Carillon, the French Commander Marquis de Montcalm had only thirty-five hundred men and a dwindling supply of rations. Shortly after he had ordered his army northward on Lake George, Abercrombie halted at Tea Island on July 5, 1758. He buried a couple of chests of valuables for safe-keeping before the impending encounter with the French. The nature and quantity of those valuables is unknown but rumored to be a fairly large treasure, possibly the payroll for Abercrombie's twelve thousand troops. After hiding this treasure trove, the army proceeded up Lake George to embark at its northern extremity and to march overland to attack the French bastion.

John Andre will be leading a party to Tea Island; I am going to persuade him to take me with him. In this way I can send information to you regarding the treasure if it is found so that you might send men to recapture it.

"Oh, my God! We found a clue! There really is a treasure on Tea Island!" Dealer's declaration was excited, and her voice shrilled. The necklace was warm and comforting around her neck. She felt *The Lady* nearby, and her lavender fragrance filled her senses with hope.

"Hey, do you smell that?" Aiden blurted out.

"Yeah, I believe I do smell something," Dex answered quizzically. "It smells like some type of flower."

"You guys smell it, too?" Dealer was flabbergasted. "I know you're going to think I'm crazy, but it is a flower. It's lavender, and I think it's *The Lady*."

Aiden shifted his position at the edge of the counter. "What makes you think it's some lady?"

"Because I've seen her before, but also in my locket there is a picture of her and Robert Townsend. At least I think he's a Townsend because he looks just like my dad," Dealer answered with slow deliberation.

Dex didn't resist the chance to make a lighthearted jab. "Are you crazy?"

"I knew you would think I was nuts, but I've seen her! She's here now. I can feel her, and I know she wants us to find the treasure," Dealer retorted more aggressively than she had intended.

A hard look came across Aiden's face. "How do you know that?"

Dealer pursed her lips and shifted her gaze. "Because the necklace I'm wearing warms up when we get close to something important. When Simcoe's around, it gets very hot. I think she's warning us to be careful."

"She's a smart lady! She doesn't like him either," Aiden murmured with grim frankness.

"Wait a minute. What necklace?" Dex still wasn't buying it.

"The one I found when I was rummaging up in the attic the other day. I've been wearing it since I discovered the trunk." Dealer lifted it from around her neck and handed it to Dex. He rubbed his thumb over the amber stone for a second, then flipped it over to inspect the locket. His face held a far-away look when he saw the couple framed within it. "Wow!" was all he could say; then he tenderly handed it back to her.

"Okay. Let's call Riley and see how she's doing with her research. Unless she's found some newspaper clipping that tells us the gold has been found, I say we go after it! After all, it may save our families from being tossed into the street." Dex's enthusiasm inspired even Dealer.

"I'm game. "How about you, Aiden?"

"Me? Sure. I don't think we have a choice; our families are desperate. Hell! The whole town is desperate," Aiden voiced with an air of defiance as he extended his arms in a gesture of emphasis. "It's getting late, though. I think Dex and I should walk Riley home from the library. I suddenly got a creepy feeling that we're being watched. Look out the window and see if you see anyone, Dex." He clearly felt uncomfortable.

"Now you're just being paranoid." Dex smirked as he pressed his hands theatrically against his chest.

"Am I?" Aiden snapped. "I've been looking out the kitchen window from time to time while you guys were reading the letter, and I'm pretty sure I saw Simcoe drive by. I don't believe it's a coincidence anymore, do you?"

Dex and Dealer looked at each other with concerned expressions. As

Aiden made his way toward the front door, the screen suddenly opened, and Dealer heard her dad bellow, "What are you doing here?"

Like cats scared by a crash, Dealer and Dex came flying out of the kitchen. They saw Aiden sheepishly walk out the door and down the steps.

"Dad!" Dealer attempted to explain. "That was completely unnecessary! Dexter and Aiden are helping me decipher the letters I found in the attic. Yesterday you said they were mine, and I decided I needed help decoding them."

Slurring his words, he briefly apologized and walked into the kitchen.

"I'm sorry."

"No need to be. I'm going to catch up with Aiden. I'll see you at school tomorrow, Dealer."

Just like that, her friends were gone, and Dealer was alone. *How could the day end like this? Everything was going fine until HE came home.* Embarrassed by the scene, Dealer made her way slowly up the stairs to her bedroom.

"Who were those boys anyway?" she heard her dad demand.

"They're friends from school. Nothing more."

"People find out you're alone in the house with boys, they'll call you a whore. What will the neighbors think?" Clearly the alcohol made him irrational.

"Well, right now I think they would say you've been drinking," Dealer growled.

"You're not getting out of this; you're grounded," he slurred.

"That's totally unfair! You're completely jumping to conclusions about me and two boys you don't even know! They were helping me with the letters; that's all! Is that really necessary?"

He turned away from her, walked into his bedroom, and slammed the door.

Dealer hadn't realized her dad had resorted to drinking early in the day. Things were going from bad to worse. She had no clue of what to say to Dex tomorrow or how she was going to handle her situation. What she did know was that she was not going to give up. Those letters were too important.

Chapter 10

DEALER DID NOT LIKE the situation. Her emotions struggled with what to do. She went back downstairs and gathered the letters off the kitchen table and shoved them into her backpack. Dragging herself up the stairs, she chucked the filled bag into the closet and flopped onto the bed. What would her friends think of her?

Dex's words played over and over in her head: "The whole town is in foreclosure." As she read over the handouts from Ms. Arnold's class, an uneasy feeling washed over her. What she read sounded more and more like the book *1984* and less and less like the friendly and easy class she had originally envisioned.

What bothered her more than anything was Ms. Arnold. It was strange how she was always rummaging through her bookshelf and rearranging books for no apparent reason. It couldn't be a coincidence that her last name was Arnold, could it? She might be wrong, but she felt that Ms. Arnold and Simcoe were somehow connected. Was he a demon or just bat shit crazy? Dealer made a mental note to ask Dex if he felt the same.

Dealer replayed that morning's English class in her head. Ms. Arnold was most definitely weird. She had spent the majority of the class period looking through notebooks stuffed in the bookcase by her desk. She remembered that Ms. Arnold had also made a point to put colored stickers on Nathan's and Elsea's backpacks without explaining why. Both kids were in Dealer's writing group, and Dealer was curious about the connection there. The fact that their last names were Hale and Darragh added a hint of mystery.

Something just was not right; things didn't fit together. Dealer would have liked to talk about her first day at school with her dad and get his opinion on Ms. Arnold, but that simply was not possible with him drunk as a skunk on who knew what. She knew he was worried about the loan payment and losing the farm so she understood the overdrinking to a slight degree, but his excessiveness and the rest of his behavior was ridiculous. How could he be so selfish? If Dealer knew drinking wouldn't solve anything, how come he didn't?

A nice warm bath was what she needed — privacy and solitude to allow her to sift through her thoughts. She filled the tub with hot water, sprinkled in some bath salts, and sank in. Old wives' tales and superstitions flittered around in her thoughts. She wiggled her toes with uneasy embarrassment that she had probably made a mountain out of a mole hill. Surely there was a rational explanation.

Dealer spent an hour trying to convince herself. It was time to call Dex to see if he was getting the same bad vibes she was about Ms. Arnold. What did he know about Nathan and Elsea, if anything? Were they distant relatives of the very people she and her friends were learning about?

She left a voice mail for Dex and hung up the phone. She couldn't get the day out of her mind. *Dex must think I'm an absolute idiot for freaking out over getting lost around the school. "Nuts" probably went through his head. I mean I even admitted to him that I saw a ghost and that the ghost is the lady pictured in my locket!*

The fact was that Dealer didn't need any more confusion or uncertainty in her life. Losing her mom and experiencing her death firsthand had been far more traumatic than she ever would have imagined. Her grandparents had treated her well, but being yanked from her dad had made her feel like an orphan. Now she was faced with losing the only stability she had left — her home. Suddenly Dealer felt like crying.

Instead she thought about the letters, the mystery of the lost gold, the bizarre teacher and banker, and her new friends, and that gave her a sense of purpose and hope.

Although she didn't want to be a newbie burden to Dex, Dealer knew it was important to speak to him about her fears and feelings. After all, he had been really nice and walked her around to all her classes, but he couldn't do that every day. More than likely she made him late to some of his own classes. Just the same, it was comforting to have someone to lean on a little again. She really didn't have the energy to figure out how to get around a school shaped like an octopus, much less decipher the letters by herself. She was no math major, but there just didn't seem to be enough codes in the letters.

Dex called back at 10:03. "Hey! Sorry I didn't call sooner, but I decided to snoop around in our basement to see if I could find any secret passages or an old trunk like the one you found. What's up?"

The sound of his voice brought Dealer back to reality and reminded her of why she'd called earlier. "Hi. I was wondering, did you notice the stickers Ms. Arnold put on Nathan's and Elsea's backpacks today?"

"No, can't say I did. Why?"

"I don' know for sure. It just seemed odd to me, and with everything that's going on, *odd* fits in nicely."

"You're right. It is odd that she would do that. Let's talk about it during lunch tomorrow."

"Sounds like a plan. I'll see you in the morning."

Physically tired and emotionally exhausted, Dealer snuggled under the covers and eventually drifted off to sleep.

Chapter 11

DEALER WOKE TO THE smell of frying bacon and was sure that her dad had gotten drunk because he had been celebrating. Hopefully he got a loan so he could get the banker off their backs and get crops planted before it was too late. One look at him told her otherwise. She was only kidding herself.

"I'm sorry, Dealer. I can't find a bank to loan me any money." Disappointment weighed heavily on his face.

Dealer wasn't ready to let him off the hook for his outburst yesterday. "But you told Grandpa you had the seeds to start planting so why don't you at least do that? Wait a minute. Do you feel okay, Dad? You don't look well."

"I'm fine, just a little headache and upset stomach. It must be from the stress." He couldn't look her in the eyes. She knew it was pure bullshit.

"Why don't you face the facts, Dad? You're drinking to the point of drunkenness. You promised me you'd stopped drinking, but you haven't kept your promise. You're drinking more than ever. You embarrassed me in front of my friends because you can't get a grip. How do you expect me to get a grip if you can't? I have to get to school so I don't have time for breakfast.

We will have to talk about this later." She scooted back her chair so hard it fell to the floor.

"I'll try a bank at East Northport. Maybe I can get some help there. If not, maybe your grandpa can loan us some money."

"It can't hurt." Dealer grabbed her backpack and slammed the door on her way out.

"You know I love you, Dealer," she heard him yell, tears stinging her eyes as she ran to the bus stop.

- - - - - - - - - - - - - -

Dex was waiting for her at the school's entrance. "Hi," he said simply.

"Hey there. Sorry about yesterday."

"Forget about it and stop apologizing; it's not your fault."

"Thanks, Dex." Dealer sighed and shrugged her shoulders, the weight of the day already heavy. "We'd better get to class."

The day seemed to fly by. The layout of the school was starting to make sense, and Dealer managed to get disoriented only once. Everyone was waiting for her by the flowering dogwood tree.

"Wow, things have really changed here at Melville High. Most of the teachers are real bitches," Aiden grunted.

"I've had the same problem all day. I've already got detention, and it's only the second day of school," Dex complained.

"So that isn't normal?" Dealer asked.

"Well, it is for me," Dex chuckled, "but not for Riley."

"What happened to you, Riley?"

"Ms. Arnold yelled at me for no reason when I was at my locker, and I yelled back. That will put your backside in detention real fast. Her house must be in foreclosure, too, because she's wound awfully tight."

By then they had reached the bus area. They agreed to check in at home and finish their homework, then meet up at the library to look for more answers.

Dealer settled in her seat at the back of the bus and pulled a letter and an old map out of her backpack. Perhaps she could find some clues to assist in decoding the message that had been written in secret so long ago. Nothing seemed to jump out at her.

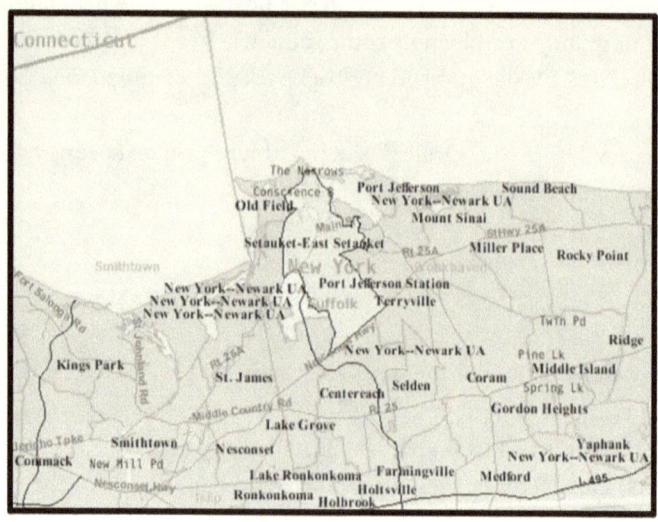

U.S. Census 2000 reference map for Setauket
(Permission Details: Public Domain)

The ride home seemed shorter than usual, and before she knew it, she was in the kitchen eating a snack, the bus's exhaust fumes still fresh in her nostrils. Her mind refused to focus on homework so she left for the library, which was far more superior. The rock on her necklace began to grow warm, and she wondered where *The Lady* was. She hadn't seen her today, yet it seemed awfully peculiar that the amber would warm up when she wasn't around.

Riley met Dealer at the library at five o'clock, and by then she was already knee deep in possible clues. Her list of tidbits about the Tea Island gold had grown quite long. "Did you find anything interesting in your search?"

"Well, maybe, but first I want to look through this last book I found, *Redcoats and Petticoats*, for historical notes or information on the ciphers." Dealer paused when she spotted Dex and Aiden coming through the library doors.

"Dex, Aiden, we're over here."

"SHHH," the librarian hissed at her.

"Hey, I just thought of an idea. How about we meet at my house this weekend and scan through my family's old Bibles for clues. They were sacred, and people used to leave lots of information in them. Maybe we can stumble upon some other codes that will help us find the lost British gold," Aiden suggested.

"You mean if someone else didn't get the treasure first," Dex mused.

"If they had, we would surely have heard about it. Riley, did you get a chance to look through the public notices in any of the recent newspapers?"

"Not yet, but I've read through a bunch of microfiche, and there's no mention of any lost gold being found. One of the librarians was helping me find a misfiled book and told me the high school is built on top of a building that was used by the British. After the War, the people of Setauket didn't want any reminders of the Redcoats so they demolished the house and buried what was left of it. Time went by, and eventually the school was built on top of its foundation."

"That's bizarre. Maybe we have a chance then," Dex speculated excitedly.

"Let's split up," Dealer suggested. "Riley, you and Aiden look for documents or books written on the history of Tea Island and see if there's any mention of ciphers we may have missed. Dex and I will head to the county courthouse and check the town's foreclosure records."

"Works for me. Let's go, Aiden." Riley prompted her friend by tugging on his sweatshirt.

Dealer was excited to investigate with Dex. She knew she was the new girl, but she truly hoped he felt something for her. God, he was cute, but she couldn't worry about romance now, even if there was such a thing. There were bigger fish to fry, namely saving their homes.

They headed down River Road toward the court-house, which was a large, ominous building surrounded by 100-year-old trees. Dex stopped abruptly and asked, "How many families do you think are in foreclosure or have recently been foreclosed upon?"

"I don't even have a guess, but we're about to find out."

The clerk of the court assisted the two researchers and showed them how to review court foreclosure files and other official records. Most of the legal descriptions they reviewed did not list addresses, but names were recorded.

"At first blush, it looks like the descendants of the Culper Spy Ring are specifically being targeted," Dex observed.

"You may be on to something with that thought." A strange look clouded Dealer's face. "But I wonder why?"

Chapter 12

THE TRIP TO THE courthouse confirmed their suspicions. Further research disclosed that all of the names of residents being foreclosed on matched names they found in the Culper Spy documents. Whatever was going on with the town, Simcoe and Ms. Arnold were definitely connected to it and involved in something sinister.

Walking through the front door, Dealer could see that her dad hadn't made it back from East Northport. She really hoped he would find someone to believe in him enough to risk placing a second mortgage on their home so he could plant crops and therefore generate some income.

Dealer paused for a second and took in the room around her. There were so many memories of her mom there. The striped black and white wallpaper hung in the kitchen, the ruffly white curtains, and her black and white polka dot apron that was still draped over the peg by the pantry door. There was the couch in the front room with its buttery folds and soft cushions that you melted into while you watched television. She couldn't help but grin at the chocolate stain on the arm of her dad's favorite recliner.

She ambled up the stairs, feeling depressed and a little nostalgic at what once was and what was never going to be again. Her mom was gone, and it was time to focus on the treasure hunt instead of herself and the possibility of losing their home. Looking at the attic door, she decided to clear the cobwebs that were forming in her mind and headed up the steep stairs. Maybe she could find another letter with a code, just maybe …

The attic usually had a dry, musty smell. She was used to it, but it gave her the willies being in the house alone. Right now she could smell lavender. She felt the hair on the nape of her neck rise, and the necklace began to warm. Turning toward the trunk, she saw *The Lady*. She beckoned Dealer to come forward with gloved hands. It was odd that she didn't feel afraid of her. *The Lady* looked wistful as she pointed to the trunk, then she was gone.

Dealer squeezed between the slats and quietly padded over to the trunk and lifted its lid, sensing today might be the day she would find something to fill in some blanks.

Stacks of letters slumped over on the floor as Dealer sifted through the trunk's contents just as she had done several times before. She decided to completely empty it. She was glad she did. Flashlight in hand, Dealer inspected the antique. She quickly discovered the maker's label on the side. The trunk had been made by London trunk maker James Bryant. A soft gasp escaped her lips when she saw the date July 6, 1773 under his name.

Completely engrossed in her exploration, Dealer did not hear the visitor who had reentered the attic nook. Instead, she inspected the lining that covered the leather, and she giggled slightly when she realized the original paper was decorated with a playing card motif. She had not stopped to think that the owner of this trunk was a person just like anybody else and enjoyed the same things.

She ran her fingers over the paper, amazed at how well it had held up after so many years. Questions filled her mind. *How many places had this trunk seen? What kinds of important papers and keepsakes had it held?*

Her heart lurched. The bottom was padded with cloth, and it appeared to have been added after its manufacture. The usual clichés about old trunks and their linings occurred to her.

It was then that Dealer felt the wisps of hair around her forehead move ever so slightly. The necklace's stone began to warm, and she looked up. *The Lady* had returned and was propped against the window sill, but she stayed only for a moment.

Dealer had the strongest feeling that she should cut away the cloth padding and sensed the urging. "What?" She wasn't sure she wanted to cut it away. This trunk was a family heirloom, her heirloom, part of her heritage. The feeling was uncomfortable, and yet somehow she knew it was necessary.

Dealer made her way to the dusty art table and scattered its contents, hoping to quickly find a pair of scissors that would work. She found some under an empty picture frame littered with what were probably mouse droppings. She cringed until she realized she was saved by the rust on the blades. They could stay there indefinitely for all she cared. She would find another way.

The button jar was probably her best bet. Dealer looked over her shoulder as she unscrewed its lid and dumped the contents on the dirty attic floor. A seam ripper had been stored there, and it was just the thing she needed to cut away the cloth without damaging it too much.

Anxious and nervous, she knelt in front of the old trunk and began carefully slitting the lining. Hesitantly she worked around the bottom and delicately sliced around the corners. There was something peeking out from inside the pocket she had just made. Not wanting to destroy the trunk any further, Dealer slowly pushed her fingers through the opening and gently pulled out a piece of parchment.

Unconcerned about the dust and dirt that would probably never wash out of her yellow pants, Dealer sat down on the floor and unfolded the document. To her surprise, it was a map of Tea Island. She recognized the code written on it and knew she and her friends could decipher it.

A letter that had been tucked within one of the map's folds fell to the floor when she finished opening it. Dealer recognized the code as having been written by General Abercrombie to John Andre. She could barely breathe. Could the clues give her the whereabouts of the scuttled treasure on Tea Island? Her excitement began to grow, and her nerves began to feel slightly jumpy.

If only she could decipher the other code, they could find the lost treasure and be closer to getting the town out of bankruptcy. She held the necklace around her neck as it glowed warm in her hands. Maybe it was a good sign.

Chapter 13

ALTHOUGH DEALER WAS EAGER to tell Dex about her find, she knew the walls of the school had ears. It would have to wait. What she needed to do instead was focus on understanding the school's layout and design so she could figure out how to get to class without being tardy.

Dex really knew his way around and agreed to give her a fully-guided tour. They sat together and made their plans before class. It made sense to her to start from the bottom up, especially since first seeing it Dealer had been curious about the mystery behind the red door in the basement.

According to Dex, the original part of the school was really old, built around 1774, and it was the first school built on Staten Island. The high grey stone turrets in all four corners of the original brick building were accessible from gated stairs on the top floor, but he said he'd only been up there once.

Dealer began the morning with a hope in her heart that today would be a better day, but she was so wrong. It turned out to be worse.

Ms. Arnold got on their case immediately, making snide remarks about each of them being little babies who were not ready for a good education. *If you ask me, she's not ready to be an educator. A torturer, yes. An educator, no way. The woman is clearly deranged. Dex and Dealer glanced at each other in disgust.*

The circumstance would have been laughable had it not been so serious. Ms. Arnold dished out verbal attacks right and left. Some of the kids looked like they would start crying or hurl at any moment. Dealer was really upset and easily embarrassed so when Ms. Arnold took the opportunity to berate her, she snapped back like a caged tiger with her claws out.

Her reaction only fed Ms. Arnold's power trip. She seemed elated in her reign of dominance over the class, and she spent half the period criticizing all of her students. Finally she decided to actually teach something and separated everyone into groups to work on a writing assignment about American Revolutionary spies.

Something gnawed in Dealer's gut, and the back of her head throbbed. Her necklace began to heat up, and when she subconsciously grabbed it, it burned her. Was this a warning? *Could Ms. Arnold be a reincarnated entity from the British gold seekers? This is just too crazy,* Dealer thought.

Nathan and Elsea were put in Dealer and Dex's group again. Nathan seemed especially nervous today and avoided eye contact. He doodled pre-calculus equations in his notebook and mumbled about the philosophical writings of Aristotle. Dealer quickly concluded that this guy either lived in another century, or he had just recently moved to Setauket.

"Moral dilemmas are the sustenance of man," Aiden speculated when Dex brought up the subject of spying.

"I think it sucks," Elsea said.

"You think what sucks?" Aiden put his chair back down on all fours and stared at her. "Moral dilemmas or men in general?"

Elsea's eyes rolled around. "Neither, moron. This class and its teacher suck."

Now she's my kind of girl, Dealer thought. Okay, she looks a little weird, but she cut right to the heart of the matter, and that's what counts. She's got my vote. It did suck, and that was the problem. How could she and her friends work on solving the Tea Island mystery and still get a passing grade from Ms. Arnold?

Dealer looked over at Dex. A slight smile played in the corners of his mouth, but he was scowling and trying to balance his pencil, point end down, on the desk.

A feeling of déjà vu engulfed Dealer, and she was just about to say something about it to Dex when Ms. Arnold slid a chair over to their table.

"So, what did you think about your assignment? Pretty cool, right?"

None of them spoke; they all just stared at her, not saying what was really on their minds. This was the first time Dealer saw her smile, and it changed her countenance. Usually she looked like the blood had been drained from her face. Now she really looked pretty, and for a second, like a nice person. But it didn't take long for her face to go cold again, her beauty vanishing almost as quickly as it had appeared. Dealer didn't trust her.

Ms. Arnold took their silence as a cue to leave and stood up. An argument was breaking out in another group so she quickly headed in their direction. They stared after her for what seemed like an eternity, confused by her audacity and absurdity.

"I'm a witch, a reincarnation of my great-great-aunt, and I'm going to put a spell on that evil woman," Elsea divulged.

Ignoring her weird comment, Dealer said, "I think we need to figure out what Ms. Arnold's problem is."

For the first time, Nathan spoke. "I think we are revisiting history."

"Okay, that sounds a bit crazy, even coming from you," Dex growled.

"I don't know, but I'm with you, Nathan. I feel like I've known all of you a lifetime, and yet I also feel like it's just beginning. I know it sounds bizarre," Riley explained.

Elsea took notice. "I told you I feel like I was born in a different time. I know we've all known each other before but under different circumstances. I recognize that necklace you're wearing, Dealer. Robert Townsend, III gave it to your great-great-grandmother who passed it down to her son and so on."

Dealer responded by clutching the necklace, and as she did, she saw *The Lady*. Beams of light shot out toward Ms. Arnold. Dealer was certain she was the only one who could see it. Mrs. Arnold hastily moved to the other side of the room but not quite fast enough. A stray beam hit its target and the slight electrical jolt caused her to trip on the foot of a desk.

"Get off me!" a classmate said as he pushed her splayed body off the top of his desk.

Ms. Arnold readjusted her blouse as she righted herself. Spittle had formed on the edge of her mouth, and she wiped it off with the back of her hand.

Nobody said a thing. The class was in a state of disbelief. There was dead silence.

The bell rang, and chairs scraped the floor as a flurry of students headed for the door. Dealer could feel a hole being burned in her back from Ms. Arnold's glare. She quickly moved in front of Dex.

"I'll see all of you on the first floor after school," Dex said as he stood in the hallway and mock saluted his friends. Then he turned on the balls of his feet and hurried out of sight.

- - - - - - - - - - - - - - -

By 3:10 most of them were gathered at the stairwell. Riley had the floor plan of the high school. They would search for an opening outside the school grounds that led to whatever was underneath the school. Dealer was beginning to get the hang of things so going down below didn't seem like such a big deal.

Aiden was the last one to show up, and he looked like he had to drag himself there. His body language told Dealer he wasn't happy about going, but everybody else was excited. They promised each other they would keep the exploration their little secret. Elsea named their "society" Culper Spy Ring 2. That took a lot of thought, Dealer groaned to herself.

They wandered around the perimeter of the school in pairs — Dealer and Dex, Aiden and Riley, and Nathan and Elsea. Just over a hill past Central Park, Dex and Dealer found a storm drain that seemed out of place. It was centered between two outcroppings of massive rocks. A short way into the tunneled area, the two discovered a red door that was locked. It looked ominous, and Dealer began to feel jittery with anxiousness. She called the other two pairs to come meet them by the tall jagged rocks. His name should be dexterity, she thought as she watched him pick the lock on the door that possibly led to an underground passage.

"Ahh, a man of many talents! How did you learn to do that?" Dealer questioned as she studied the movements of his fingers and wrist.

"Don't ask if you don't really want to know."

"Well, I do want to know but not now."

The lock released. The tunnel looked old and creepy. It was obvious that it was man-made, tube shaped, and pitch black. In unison, they turned on their cell phones' flashlight apps so they could see. Dealer didn't know what was worse — seeing all the cobwebs surrounding them or the uneven ground that promised a fall.

They walked in tandem down the passageway until they heard the football team practicing above them. This meant they were approaching the old house where the school had been built on top of it.

Up ahead, another path veered off to the left, and water trickled down the sides of the walls. Dealer knew from the dank smell that there was water before they actually saw it. Without warning, a loud, agonizing scream pierced the air. Everyone but Dex turned to run, but he didn't hesitate. He quickened his pace forward. Recognizing his conviction, they quickly changed their minds and followed him.

Just ahead a wooden stairway led down to the depths below. There was the sense that everyone of them wanted to bolt. Nathan looked like he was about to crawl under a rock. Dealer watched as Elsea took his hand and tugged him forward down a magnificent golden stairway. Even though they were tip-toeing, every step on the marble stairs sounded like a rap on a bongo drum.

The smell of mildew permeated the air, and the more stairs they descended, the stronger it became. It felt like nobody had been down there in a million years, but where did the scream come from?

The walls of a once-grand home were tiled all the way to the ceiling, and they were covered with splashes of green growth that resembled some long-forgotten science project. They traveled slowly, almost reverently, down the stairs to the deepest, most mysterious part of the underground home. At the bottom of the second flight of stairs, there was a small landing with two metal scrolled doors fitted with ornate shiny brass doorknobs.

"Look how shiny the doorknobs are; if no one has been down here in a long time, wouldn't they be tarnished?" Nobody acknowledged that Dealer had spoken. They didn't want to let on that they were terrified.

Dealer decided to keep quiet. Immediately Dex held up his hand to signal the group to stop moving. They stopped dead in their tracks and listened. Muffled voices came from the hallway to the right; it sounded like a chant of some sort, and there was some faint moaning. Dex motioned them in the opposite direction, and they hurried down the dim corridor and through an old wooden door. They gravitated to the far wall as he quietly closed the door. They discovered they were huddled in an old library as their eyes gradually adjusted to the darkness that surrounded its dank walls.

"Someone is down here. I can hear voices."

"No one is supposed to be here," Riley said, shivering as she informed them of information of which they were well aware.

"We are," Nathan said quietly.

Dex ignored him. "All of you stay here. I'll be back in a minute."

"Oh, no, that's not happening," Dealer quickly interjected. She was not about stay in that spooky room, and neither was anyone else. Even in the dimness it was evident that Nathan's face was a pale white. Elsea was mumbling to herself and making weird arm movements. Maybe she was casting a spell or something; Dealer hoped it was something to protect them all.

They left the safety of the darkness and moved in the direction of the voices. This part of the hall was tiled like the stairs, but they glowed as if there was some kind of light behind them. Dealer wondered if there was a hidden room on the other side. It was kind of eerie because although there were no lights to guide them, they could still see their way clearly without using their cell phones.

Dex stopped abruptly, and Dealer ran into him. They had reached a huge round marble column that partially blocked their view, but she could see that this was a large, old parlor. The walls were white marble, and marble columns that looked like they were holding up the multi-colored glass ceiling towered above the room. Simcoe and Ms. Arnold were sitting side by side at a table, but instead of their unusually white skin, it appeared to be a bloated, ruddy, purplish color.

"Arnold and Simcoe?" Dex whispered as he turned to his friends.

"Oh, my God!" Aiden gasped.

"What are they doing down here?" Dealer squeezed Dex's hand to get his attention, but he just squeezed hers harder in an effort to silence her. It worked. She was scared shitless. The amber in her necklace grew hot, warning her. She knew they had to get out of there fast.

"What are they doing, Dex?" she whispered.

"I don't know what they're doing, but I'm sure it's no good."

"We need to get out of here; something is very wrong," Elsea pressed, clearly agitated.

Dealer could smell lavender all around them. *The Lady* was there. A gust of wind picked up, but there weren't any windows. It urged them back the way they came.

Simcoe and Ms. Arnold suddenly stood up from the table and walked toward the back of the room. No one had noticed the gated cell that Simcoe was now unlocking. Their backs to the parlor, they hovered around, making strange motions and gurgling sounds.

"Shhh. Be quiet!" Dex demanded in a whisper.

Ms. Arnold shifted her position. "Look, there is a woman lying on a table! I can see a needle in her arm, and blood is coming out of a hose, and — oh, my God, Simcoe and Ms. Arnold are drinking it!" Aiden was so shaken by the sight, he forgot to whisper. His voice echoed off the tiled walls, and immediately the two fiends jerked around.

The teens didn't wait to see what would happen. Dealer grabbed Nathan's hand and pulled him up where he had been crouching, and they raced down the hallway behind the others, not caring about noise. Up the stairs they raced, almost trampling each other in their haste. They finally reached the entrance, and when they hit the dark night, they didn't even stop to close the door.

Dealer noticed that Nathan had peed his pants; she hoped no one else had.

Chapter 14

BOLTING OUT OF THE outcropping of rocks, they ran, the chilled night air forcing their lungs to breathe as they collapsed in unison at the edge of the football field.

"Okay, that was just plain scary," Dealer shouted over the pounding of her heart.

"Yeah! I don't believe what I just saw," Dex stuttered as he gasped for breath.

"I'm glad we didn't stay for the finale." Elsea draped her arms over her knees. Even that didn't stop the shaking.

"Are they for real?" Riley was angry. "Those people need to be stopped!"

"I think we are in way over our heads; something bad is about to happen," Nathan protested.

"This sounds weird, but I think they're here because they don't have a choice. There's a reason they are drinking blood. Maybe it gives them some sort of power. That lady strapped on the marble altar was just plain freaky! There has to be an explanation for that." Elsea slowly caught her breath. She was doing her best to convince herself that they had just had a run-in with some sort of weirdness, but she couldn't explain it.

"We should consider calling the cops because I think that lady is being held against her will. Nobody willingly allows themselves to be strapped to a table or altar or whatever the hell that thing was she's on. No matter what, we have to be very careful. I'm sure Simcoe suspects that we're on to them. He's been following us, and there's a reason why." Dex spoke with precision.

"That's a no brainer — the gold. Ms. Arnold and Mr. Simcoe want that treasure, and they're convinced we know something about it. It doesn't take an Einstein to figure out that we've been researching that history. Maybe they failed to find it before and couldn't stop the British from losing the war. Maybe they were cursed to come back here and try again," Dealer elaborated as she regarded Dex critically.

Aiden was visibly shaken from the encounter in the underground room. "Let's get out of here. There's nothing to stop them from following us here, and who knows what they are capable of."

Riley's gaze steadily scanned the field. "I have an idea, but I need one more look in the Setauket library. I just remembered something I saw there, and if I hurry I can make it before they close."

"You're not going alone," Aiden insisted. "I'll go with you."

- - - - - - - - - - - - - - -

Walking through town with Dex, Elsea, and Nathan gave Dealer a sense of belonging. Seeing the quaint houses and stately buildings in the old Setauket Historic District confirmed that she was here to stay, and she was going to find the gold on Tea Island. This is what their forefathers fought and died for, and she wasn't going to let them down. She had a sense that they were depending on her, but she wasn't sure why.

"What's that huge rock?" she asked, pointing with enthusiasm to a big hunk of ten by twenty foot rock that was so massive she could see it in the woods.

"It's called the Patriot's Rock; it's where General Holden Parson hid with his men until they finally withdrew after three hours of gunfire and headed back to Connecticut. Back then there were no woods so can you imagine that monster sitting on the Green? If you look at the Village Green, you'll see a bunch of stray bullets from that stand-off are embedded in the walls of the Caroline Church of Brookhaven." Nathan was a walking encyclopedia and never missed a moment to share his knowledge of history.

"Look! There's Riley and Aiden; they look scared." Elsea inclined her head toward the library.

The four of them jogged over just as their friends came down the library steps. One look at their faces told Dex something was up. "What's wrong?"

"I'm so relieved to see you guys!" Riley said almost breathlessly. "You won't believe what we discovered! Let's go somewhere else so we can talk without company. These walls have ears, and I think Simcoe is following me."

Dex grabbed her elbow. "Don't look back; he's coming through the door right now, and he looks pissed off."

"Well, I know why," Aiden said. "If you're all game, I want to go to the cemetery. The tombstones may hold some clues."

"My mom won't let me go there; she says bad people hang out in cemeteries. I've got to go home; I'm scared." Dealer noticed that Nathan was genuinely afraid. "When I get home, I'll call the police and tell them that I saw a lady strapped to a table down in the basement of the school."

"Good idea, Nathan. The cemetery can wait. Be careful walking home," Elsea insisted, concern shadowing her face.

"I will. It's not dark yet so I'll cut through Village Green along Lake George."

"Just to be safe, Riley and I will walk you part way home in just a minute, but first you need to hear this." Aiden pushed himself in the center. "Simcoe is responsible for all the homes in foreclosure that belonged to the descendants of the Culper Spy Ring. He may have seemed creepy before, but it's obvious that he's definitely got a plan up his sleeve."

"Oh, shit! That means it's all of our families," Dealer gasped.

"I have a headache," Elsea moaned. "This is all too much to take in."

- - - - - - - - - - - - - -

Aiden and Riley walked Nathan halfway home and then ran back to town at breakneck speed. By the time Dealer and Dex saw them crossing the Village Green, they were completely out of breath.

"Why are you two running? Save your breath for God's sake!" Dex scolded.

"Are you kidding me? If we're dead, we won't need any breath!" Aiden heaved. "It's nearly dark, and we saw Simcoe talking on his cell phone after we left Nathan near his house. Simcoe started walking toward us at a fast pace. We ran all the way back to warn you guys."

"Did you hear who he was talking to?" Dealer realized the inquiry was a stupid one.

"No, he was too far away. Did you hear anything, Riley?"

"No, I didn't hang around long enough to care. He disappeared into the trees not far from the Presbyterian Church cemetery on the hill."

"By any chance did you find out anything else while you were at the library?" Elsea took a gamble and asked.

"Yeah, as a matter of fact, I did. As far as I can tell, every single one of the homes in foreclosure by Simcoe's bank was owned by our great-grandparents. At least the names are the same."

Dex raised his eyebrows. "All of them?"

"Well, not all. Some homes were destroyed, and some of the original families moved away. But the farms owned by the original ring are in the process of foreclosure," Riley explained further.

A bystander could have heard a pin drop. "So all of our relatives were part of the Culper Ring?" Dealer asked.

"Yes, Robert Tallmadge developed The Culper Spy Ring out of necessity in an effort to thwart the Red Coats. British spies infiltrated Washington's patriots, and troops ambushed them as they went to stop the British from advancing. Tallmadge's spy ring countered British activities. Most, if not all, of the members were from Setauket, Tallmadge's home town," Aiden told us.

"I know a little about the Culper Ring," Elsea added. "From 1778 to 1781, this group from Setauket was formed to pass information about the British Troops' movements from New York City to Washington. The spy ring consisted primarily of Setauket residents, including Tallmadge, Robert Townsend, Caleb Brewster, and an important agent named Abraham Woodhull."

"Hannah Woodhull lives down the street from me," Dealer interjected.

"The Culper Ring was successful in alerting Washington about various plots, including surprise attacks on the newly-allied French Troops, a scheme to counterfeit the Continental Army currency, and the secret defection of a very important general in the Continental Army. I remember a lot of information from some of the letters you found in the trunk, Dealer. During the occupation of the British in Setauket, residents held religious services at the Caroline Church while the British forces occupied the Presbyterian Church. The pulpit of the Presbyterian Church was destroyed, and gravestones surrounding the church were moved as part of the British fortification. The pastor was our relative, Robert Tallmadge's father and one of Dex's ancestors. He was murdered by Lt. Simcoe. He must be the same guy or his ghost who is following us around."

"You won't find any of that information in our history books," Elsea said.

"They kept their promise to keep the members of the group secret," Riley continued. "They were known only by numbers; some of them didn't even know who was a spy and who wasn't. It was quite ingenious."

"Less chance of being discovered that way, or if they were captured and tortured, they couldn't identify who another spy was," Aiden pointed out.

"It's getting late, and I have a lot of homework to do for Ms. Arnold's class. Since Nathan is in our group, I want to make sure he understands everything and doesn't get picked on any more than is absolutely necessary. He was so embarrassed today. He's really a smart kid but shy and a little too trusting," Dealer commented.

"Yeah, I can already hear her tearing him down for looking sloppy, just like his poor parents," Aiden said, half mocking Ms. Arnold.

"She even ripped on his mom for not being very smart, saying no wonder they were in financial trouble — right in front of the class," Dex recalled. "Wait, look at this list. Is Nathan Hale's family name on it, Riley?"

"Let me check. Yeah, poor kid. That family just can't catch a break. Not long ago their farm was set on fire, but no one knows who did it. During the summer their barn was burned down, and they lost all the hay to feed their cows. They had to sell their herd at a discount just to save the farm."

"Who bought the cows?" Dealer asked.

"Ms. Arnold did."

"Wow!" was all she could say. Without another word, Dealer headed home, walking along Lake George, listening to the sound of the water rushing to shore as the tide came in. It was soothing to her. She could feel the presence of *The Lady* by her side, the necklace's stone becoming almost too hot. Lost in her thoughts, the beat-up suitcase on the water's edge didn't register at first. Something about it pushed through, and she stopped to look at it.

Suddenly an arm grabbed her. She began to scream, but as she whirled around, she realized that it was Dex. He leaned forward, and she was so scared she leaned back into him. His warmth and his kindness radiated against her skin. Slowly he leaned over, lowered his head, and kissed her gently.

"I think we are all afraid of what is going on and who Simcoe and Arnold really are," he said, breaking the moment. "I wanted to make sure you were okay."

"Dex," Dealer said breathlessly, "do you think Simcoe and Arnold are some type of evil spirits?" She instantly felt stupid for asking the question.

"I'm not sure, but what would a reincarnated spirit need with money?" He held her hand for just a moment more.

"Maybe it's not the money that's important. Maybe it's something else that was left undone that brought them back," Dealer said after a pause.

"Maybe they never left," Dex fired back.

Dealer felt the hair on her neck rise, and the necklace became hot on her chest once again as she turned to say goodbye to Dex. If she hadn't been in such a hurry to get home and think about that kiss, curiosity would have gotten the best of her, and she would have pulled that suitcase out of the water for a closer look. But it was late, and her dad would be home by now. She hoped he had gotten a loan, and the pizza he had promised for dinner would be on the table.

Chapter 15

WALKING THROUGH THE GATE of the white picket fence, Dealer felt a sense of dread. She looked at the old tire swing her dad had made for her on her seventh birthday. It hung from the old oak tree where her childhood best friend Taylor and she had carved their names inside a heart. She stood and watched the cool breeze blow it gently back and forth. Slowly she walked over to their beat up pick-up truck, and after laying her hands on the hood, she knew her dad hadn't visited the bank. It was stone cold.

Tears clouded her eyes as she ran up the steps and pushed the screen door open. "Dad! Dad!" She found him passed out on the couch. Beer bottles littered the coffee table. The stale smell of alcohol hung in the air, and a feeling of defeat settled in Dealer's stomach.

Disgusted, she bolted to her bedroom and slammed the door. Pizza and dinner forgotten, she rocked back and forth, the teddy bear her mom had given her before she died clutched tightly to her chest. Dealer's life seemed hopeless. She fell into an anxious sleep, scenes from the car accident flooding her dreams.

The firefighters pulled her through the window, but they struggled to remove Nancy's body from the wreckage. She was stuck, crushed by the roof of the car and the impact into the tree and embankment. From the gurney Dealer saw her behind the steering wheel. In her dream she held the necklace that she had found in the upstairs attic trunk. Her mom's eyes pleaded with her, telling her the necklace had some purpose. The face faded away, and in its place was the man who had laughed at her while she was stuck in the car. Simcoe. Dealer woke up shaking, sweat pouring out of every crevice of her body.

- - - - - - - - - - - - - -

The next morning Dealer woke to the sound of Dad banging around in the kitchen. A cabinet door shut with a thump. She walked in cautiously, uneasy about his likely condition and mood.

"I'm sorry, Dealer," her dad began sheepishly. "The bank declined to loan me any more money. I have no excuse; it's over." He continued making a breakfast of bacon and eggs.

Dealer visibly stiffened. "You didn't even go to the bank yesterday, did you? You chose to get drunk instead. I can smell it on you. You made a promise to me, Dad — a promise you didn't keep. Can't you please just stop and get a clue? Forget breakfast for me. I'm going to school." She yanked up her backpack.

Suddenly there was a rush of cold air and a movement up the stairs. Dealer pushed aside the temptation to check it out. The attic's mystery had to wait until later. She softened a little. It was a difficult time for both of them. "We can talk about this tonight. I'm sure you'll figure out a way to save the farm if you stop drinking long enough. You've always come through before, Dad."

He smiled a weak smile and looked at her, tears filling his eyes. "I'll try a bank in another county; maybe I can get help there. I'm thinking I should go to an AA meeting while I'm out of town. I need help, baby girl. I don't seem to be managing very well on my own."

"See, I knew you'd come up with a great idea! I love you, Dad." She proudly walked out the back door.

"I love you, Dealer; you're the reason I keep trying!"

"I know, Dad. I know."

Chapter 16

DEALER WAS EAGER TO get home. When the final bell rang. she rushed ahead of the herd of kids and ran to catch her bus. It would have been nice to visit with her friends, but she was embarrassed. She felt hopeless because her dad felt hopeless. Even if the treasure was found and the homes in town saved from foreclosure, her dad would still be the town drunk. Dealer was ready to give up. She didn't know how much more she could take.

Dex came running up just before she got on the bus. As if he knew what she was thinking, he encouraged her. "It'll be okay, Dealer; hang in there a little longer." She smiled weakly and got on the bus, promising to meet everybody later at the library.

No sooner had she settled into her seat when the thought occurred to her that she didn't have to go home yet. Her dad wouldn't be back. She could use this time to further investigate the mysteries beneath the school. It might be the place to find long lost clues. Did Robert Townsend, her great-great-grandfather, know *The Lady*? Had he been married to her?

Quickly she exited the bus. At that moment it dawned on her that she hadn't seen Nathan in class, nor had the police shown up at school. Maybe he had lost his nerve to call them and reveal that they had been in a place they shouldn't have been. But where was he? Was he too scared to even go to school? Events were becoming more odd and curious by the minute.

Dealer stood at the corner and looked around. Mr. Simcoe drove by, slowing as he passed, his eerie stare making her skin crawl. As if sensing some danger, the rock on her necklace began to grow warm. She wondered if *The Lady* was speaking to her, trying to get her attention. She knew she needed to heed its warning, but she could not convince herself to do so. The tunnel was too big of a draw for her.

Dealer found her way back to the copse of trees. Picking the lock like Dex had done, she quietly walked through the tunnel and down the staircase to the parlor. Sure enough, Ms. Arnold was there. Dealer ducked behind one of the large marble columns, her heart pounding almost uncontrollably. She hadn't really planned on seeing anybody. Reassuring small noises that meant her nemesis was preoccupied gave her the courage to cautiously peer around the side.

Ms. Arnold was holding a lens and some old microfiche she must have confiscated from the library, inspecting it very carefully. Boy, was Ms. Wright, the librarian, going to be pissed about that! Dealer thought. Microfiche was old and valuable because it carried information as far back as when the library had been built.

Ms. Arnold placed the sheet of film on the table and turned around. Dealer instinctively moved back behind the safety of the huge pillar. Her necklace became hot, and Ms. Arnold walked past. Dealer didn't dare move. There was nowhere to run if she was discovered. Fear gripped her. What if

Ms. Arnold had an overly keen sense of smell or of presence? She shouldn't have come by herself, but it was too late.

Slowly Dealer edged around the pillar away from Ms. Arnold's view. If anybody else was in the parlor, she would be seen. She hugged the column tightly with her back, hoping she could blend right into its surface. She searched the surrounding area for another place to hide as best she could without even turning her head. Nothing seemed promising.

The amber pulsated against her skin. Dealer slightly turned the way she thought *The Lady* was pulling her. She realized Ms. Arnold was nowhere to be seen, and for a brief moment the coast was clear.

Dealer's flight mechanism kicked in, and she wove past the salon into another damp, dark chamber. Somewhere the sound of running water broke the silence. She began to shiver and instinctively wrapped her arms around herself to ward off the cold. An old chair was laying on the ground, and Dealer managed to trip over it. Frozen in place, she lay still, rubbing her shin and hoping Ms. Arnold hadn't noticed the noise.

Then she heard it — a moaning sound coming from deeper inside the chamber. A part of her wanted to see what it was, but the stone had grown cold against her chest, and adrenalin took over. What would happen if she was discovered? She was momentarily distracted by a piece of wadded up paper by the chair's leg. She grabbed it and slowly rose to her feet to get her bearings. A blood-curdling scream resonated through the air, and she nearly fell again. Panic set in. Dealer tore up the stairs and out the door as if her life depended on it and didn't stop running until she was almost home. She was shaking uncontrollably.

She thought Simcoe and Ms. Arnold were still holding someone captive in their underground chamber. Was she imagining things? Was it a recording, or was it real? If it was real, who was it, and what kind of torture were they using and why? Where was Nathan? Maybe he never had the chance to call the police. Dealer knew they needed help, but whom could she trust?

Finally she caught her breath and realized her hand still clutched the piece of paper. She placed it on her knee and smoothed out the wrinkles. It appeared to be faded cipher.

O Never says that I was false of Heart
William Shakespeare
Though distance seemed my flame to qualify as easy
might I from myself depart
As from my soul which in thy breath doth lie.
That is my home of love; if I have ranged,
642 GPMKRJ uiphcpa nip vq yiuvrqcpv
Like him that travels I return again,
Just to the time, not with the time exchanged,
So that myself bring water for my stain.
vq veoi 440 uvpevgcei rqucvcqp
Never believe though in my nature reined
All frailties that besiege all kinds of blood,
bwhuqp
That I could so preposterously be stained
Mquv 223 433 vie cumeph
To love if nothing all they so in of good I call;
For nothing this wide universe
Save thou, my rose, in it though art my all.

What did the letters and numbers mean? She headed home, wary of every movement around her. Relief flooded over her when she walked through the screen door. She double-checked the lock. She rummaged through the side table drawer in the living room and found her dad's magnifying glass. Grabbing a Coke and a pocket pizza, she wormed her way onto a kitchen chair. It was time to see if the paper held other clues that were not noticeably perceptible to the naked eye. While there appeared to be faded areas that might mean something, Dealer couldn't be sure. This was going to take a long time, and she needed her friends to help her.

Her dad pulled up in the driveway before she could dial Riley's number. What should she expect? Should she disappear before he came through the door to save herself the agony? There wasn't enough time. Surprise was in order because he looked better than she had seen him look in a long, long time.

He was trying to contain himself, but it was impossible. He wrapped his arms around Dealer and held her tight. "Dealer, I explained my situation to Sybil Ludington, the bank manager at a bank in Weber County, and when she heard that I was from Setauket and that our farm was being foreclosed on by Simcoe, she immediately had me complete an application. Then she drew up the papers!"

Dealer could feel his grin through her hair. "Dad, that's so great! I knew you could find somebody to help us! I knew it! It also sounds like she may know something about what's going on with all the foreclosures in this town!"

"Maybe so. I didn't stand around and discuss it with her! I headed straight home to tell you the good news."

"I'm really glad you did! Do you want some pizza?"

"Actually, that does sound good. I'm starving! But something else happened, Dealer. I went to an AA meeting and got a sponsor. I'm not going to kid you, though; things are going to be tough now and again."

"Well, you took the first step, and that's where you have to start if you're going to get yourself sober and stay sober. I'm so proud of you! I know it hasn't been easy."

"It hasn't been easy on either of us," he admitted, "but I promise I'll take life one day at a time. I'm going to make this work for us."

"Would you like to see the cipher I found in the library, Dad?" she asked excitedly.

The microwave's bell dinged, and as she reached in to get the pizza, her Dad moved the paper across the table to look at it. Using the magnifying glass to scan it, he blurted out, "I recognize this name from one of our old family photo albums. Wait here a minute, Dealer, and I'll go get the book."

Dealer had no idea of how happy she could feel until that moment, and she was happy! There was a good chance that she had her dad back, and maybe they could get a crop in the ground before spring. She truly hoped so.

"Look, it's pretty old so handle it carefully, Dealer. I can tell you're anxious." He returned to the kitchen table.

It was true; Dealer was anxious! She could hardly wait to get her hands on that book! She wanted to snatch it right out of his hands, but she restrained herself and waited for him to pass it to her. It was wrapped in faded blue cloth and loosely bound. The paper was made of old parchment, and the tintype photos of relatives that had been printed on it were faded around the edges. Dealer couldn't believe there was a picture of the Culper Spy Ring inserted between the pages, and her dad had kept a copy. "What name do you recognize, Dad?"

"Well, my own, of course, but also Lydia Darragh. I remember Great-Grandpa speaking fondly of Agent 355 when he was lucid. He had dementia and had to be placed in an old folk's home. When he was delirious, he spoke of her in sorrow and cried. In his sleep he talked of lost love, gold, and maps. I never thought anything of it — just thought they were the ravings of an old man, but maybe I was wrong. The trunk you found in the attic proves there is something to what he was saying; maybe there is lost gold. Long ago my aunts and uncles used to talk a lot about my great-grandfather. From what I understand, he was pretty promiscuous. Maybe Lydia and Great-Grandpa had an affair," he speculated. "Can I look at the cipher that reads 355?"

"Sure but why?"

"Look under this caption of Lydia Darragh. It was written by Robert; it read, 'My love, 355, you will live forever in my heart.' That kind of changes history for us, don't you think?" He pursed his lips and continued, "It also gives us the name of the very important person who spied for Robert Tallmadge and George Washington. She turned the tides on Benedict Arnold and the capture of West Point College.

"I remember a little of the history of that event and the capture of John Andre. Let me go get that book. It's called *Washington's Spies*," he said as he left the kitchen.

Moments later he returned with the book in his hand. He flipped carefully through its pages. "In this book it states that John Andre was born in 1760, the son of a cold Swiss merchant and an exuberant Parisian mother. He grew up in Geneva but after training in languages, music, dance, and mathematics, left for London to work in his father's firm. Thankfully, when he was nineteen, Andre's father died, and he inherited a nice little fortune, thereby relieving him of the burden of labor. He got engaged to an Anna Seward, but she broke it off, believing he lacked, and I quote, 'the reasoning mind she required'."

"Wow, that was kind of cold."

Her dad went on, "Bored and newly single, Andre bought a second lieutenant's commission in a smart regiment, the Royal Welch Fusiliers, but transferred as a full lieutenant to the Seventh Foot, which was headed for

Quebec in late 1775. He was taken as a prisoner during the siege of Fort Saint-Jean shortly thereafter. Andre charmed his captors and was traded in a prisoner exchange after the Battle of New York in 1776. He soon became a staff officer at General Howe's headquarters, serving as a translator for the Hessian troops. When his benefactor left for England, he joined Sir Henry Clinton's staff. Clinton took a liking to him, and Andre became the British commander's first friend and confidant. In three short years, he had advanced from being a mere servant in the Fusiliers to Clinton's adjunct general, the eighteenth century equivalent of a chief-of-staff.

"In many respects Captain John Andre resembled Captain Nathan Hale; both were gentlemen and graceful, artistic, and talented. It also happens that both, too, were unsuited for espionage. Andre once admitted that he, like Hale, was 'too little accustomed to duplicity' to succeed in the game. The Andre-Arnold correspondence mirrored what passed between the Culper Ring and its manager — manifold examples of crossed wires, elementary mistakes, and petty irritations.

"Both groups of men used an alpha-numeric substitution code, Tallmadge's being based on his own code dictionary and Andre's on William Blackstone's Legal Commentaries, a book which he and Arnold possessed. Soon after making contact, they began using it as the common sourcebook. 'Three numbers made up a word,' instructed Andre. 'The first is the page, the second the line, and the third the word.' So general — which could be found in Blackstone's book on page 35, at the twelfth line, eight words from the left — became 35.12.8. Pretty intriguing, don't you think?"

"I wonder if Benedict Arnold knew that his wife Peggy was having an affair with Andre?" Dealer asked.

"I doubt it," her dad said, flipping to another page. "If he did, I think he would have ditched her and left her to fend for herself in America; instead she escaped with him to Britain."

There was more. "In some of their correspondences, as Townsend did with his letter to 'Colonel Floyd,' Andre and Arnold disguised the real meaning of their words with harmless poems, talks of the weather, a business deal between two crooked merchants, or the complex affairs of an old woman's health. Andre, like Tallmadge with Woodhull, cajoled and chided his secret spy, though — unlike his American counterpart — he did not trust him, and it took several months of Arnold's persuasion to stumble upon a bona fide, highly-placed, and voluntary mole. The difference between Arnold and the Culper Ring, of course, is that Benedict Arnold was a mercenary entrepreneur, continually demanding more money for his treasury while Andre tried to gauge how fertile his man's supply of intelligence was likely to be.

"Andre was perfectly blunt about his decision — dispatched to and from foreign courts original documents, intimation of channels through which intelligence passes, taking possession of a considerable seaport, and defeating the troops assigned to the defense of the province. Andre asked Arnold at one point if he could obtain the command in Carolina, but Benedict Arnold offered up West Point. In the continual request of Arnold's pleas for money, Andre remained businesslike, telling his spy that services done are the terms on which we promise reward, in these you see we are profuse; we conceive them proportion to the risk." Dad stopped his history lesson when a knock sounded on the kitchen door.

"Oh, hi, Aiden. How are you?" Dealer stood back from the door as invitation for him to come in. He was holding an old Bible and a letter.

"I thought maybe this could help. I found it in our basement, and it was written by Lydia Darragh's son," he said as he walked through the door.

Chapter 17

"IT SEEMS PROMISING," AIDEN said as his gaze shifted from Dealer to her dad. "Hello, Mr. Townsend."

"Well, hello, Aiden." Mr. Townsend rose to greet him with a handshake. "What do you have there?"

"I found a letter written by Robert Townsend to a lady in this Bible. According to the letter, Agent 355 was a beautiful young girl with long silver blonde hair and midnight blue eyes who assisted as a nurse, midwife, and even as an undertaker to help her family survive the cold, harsh winters." Aiden pushed the thin paper toward Dealer.

Mr. Townsend's expression lit up. "Can I add a little here? Lydia was raised by a strong, intelligent woman who came from a wealthy Dublin, Ireland family to the Americas. She was a Quaker and didn't believe in war. She had also seen many of her friends forced out of their homes when General Howe decided to make his headquarters there."

"My God! If they had been displaced," Dealer interjected angrily, "those women found themselves at risk of rape by the occupying armies!" She continued on, telling the two about how Lord Rawdon and the Fifth Foot Infantry Regiment gang raped three American women a few weeks before the Battle of Long Island. One was a woman in her seventies, another was pregnant, and the other was a young girl. "What they did to them was brutal," she concluded with a deep breath.

"That is no way to treat a woman, even in war," Aiden proclaimed.

"I totally agree." Dealer's dad frowned in thought.

Aiden continued explaining the letter. "When the officers began having their meetings, Agent 355, without any training on how to carry out spy activities, decided to snoop around. She sent anything she learned about General Howe and John Andre's meetings to her brother, who was in George Washington's army at Whitemarsh.

"Lydia made up her own code regarding the information she gathered; she wrote it on tiny pieces of paper and put them inside cloth-covered buttons. She then sewed the buttons on her coat and traveled to Washington's camp, selling eggs from her chickens. This young, beautiful girl whose parents housed John Andre became an expert at crossing British lines. She was very innocent looking and extremely convincing as a naïve young lady who sold her eggs to soldiers while her mother helped birth babies for the Americans and the English."

"Man, she was good!" Dealer laughed as she took in the measure of *The Lady*'s resolve.

"Well, if you think that's good, there's more, Dealer." Aiden paused, then continued. "Agent 355 made her way to her brother Charles, who helped her cut the buttons off. As soon as he read the secret notes, she sewed the buttons back on."

"She was either crazy or terribly brave." Dealer could not help herself. Her excitement continually interrupted. "But go on."

Aiden slightly rolled his eyes in frustration. He picked up where he left off. "Washington knew that Howe was going to attack him in Whitemarsh because of the intelligence Agent 355 had given to her brother so he devised a plan and gave it in the form of a note to a man whom he knew was spying for Howe. The man immediately delivered it to Howe. The note told Howe that Gates, one of George Washington's men, was traveling to Philadelphia with 8,000 men. It was imperative that General Howe keep his Redcoats in Philadelphia so they wouldn't lose the city.

"As part of the deception, Washington ordered three of his generals who had troops near New York to pretend as if they were preparing to invade New York. They were also told to make sure that their 'secret' was divulged to traitors of the Americans.

"General Howe believed the disinformation and stayed in Philadelphia, which gave Washington time to dig in at Whitemarsh and Tallmadge time to train his spies.

"Lydia continued to pass information to her brother. One evening John Andre came to Lydia and asked that she and her family go to bed early so that no one would be around when he and his men used the parlor that evening. The Redcoats arrived around eight o'clock that night. Sensing the importance of this meeting, Agent 355 tiptoed into a hidden closet and eavesdropped on the conversations. She heard Howe's top officers discussing what sounded like a plan for a surprise attack on Washington's army. At one point she heard an officer reading the direct order for British troops to march from the city of Philadelphia at dawn on December 3rd and head for Whitemarsh."

"What did she do? Did she get away with it?"

Aiden leaned his elbows on the table and continued, "Agent 355 slipped into her bedroom and made believe she was asleep. After the meeting, Andre knocked on the doors of the family members repeatedly until everyone came out but Lydia. Finally Lydia came to the door sleepily. Convinced that no one in the family had been wandering around during the secret meeting, Andre went back to his headquarters."

"Great! She did make it! I can't believe she wasn't caught," Dealer said in awe. "That would not have been good for her if she had been!"

"You're right about that. That would have been a tragedy for sure," Dad suggested. "Lydia left her home on December 1st and went to Howe's headquarters and asked her cousin for a pass so she could travel to a flour mill outside the city."

Dad continued on with information he had pulled from the old scrapbook he had found. "She trudged for hours through the snow, carrying an empty flour sack. Shortly before she reached the Rising Sun Tavern just north of Philadelphia, she met a member of the Pennsylvania militia and told Tallmadge what she had heard the night before. He said he would take her report immediately to Washington.

"The innkeeper was a sympathizer and filled her bag with flour as she took out a note sewn in the lining of her coat and handed it to Tallmadge. Upon unrolling the paper Tallmadge found information that General Howe was coming out the next morning with 5,000 men, 13 cannons, baggage wagons, and 11 boats on wheels. He compared it with other information he had, then immediately set out for Washington's headquarters.

"While preparing to leave the tavern, he was warned that the British cavalry were nearby. Stepping to the door he saw them chasing his patrols at full speed. Tallmadge leaped onto his saddle, hoisted up Agent 355, and they galloped off to Setauket where he left her in the care of his friend Robert Townsend."

"Is that when they fell in love?" Dealer wondered out loud.

"Dealer, stop interrupting!" Aiden nudged her kindly but impatiently. "You're such a romantic! I can tell you this: Lydia continued to spy for Washington with the help of Robert Townsend. She told him of secret meetings and about all the men who attended Andre's meetings. One man she discovered was Benedict Arnold. Robert Townsend reported this, and John Andre was captured. Arnold escaped and became a Brigadier General for the Redcoats. Before he fled for England he had the pregnant Lydia Darragh captured and put on the death ship, the HMS Jersey. After giving birth to a son, Robert II, Lydia died sometime later aboard the ship from complications of childbirth. Thousands of others died of starvation on the disease-infested ship. Robert Townsend was never the same."

"That is so tragic," Dealer's dad said as he sighed a heavy sigh.

"It is so sad, yes." Dealer hesitated, then picked up where her dad left off. "According to a letter written by Robert's brother, Robert never spoke of his service, never applied for a pension, never corrected those who assumed he had done nothing but tend his farm during the war, and never, it seems, recovered emotionally from the death of his beloved wife, Agent 355, captured and imprisoned. He kept to himself, staying near his brothers and their families, and he never remarried. One day he found a large, blond, blue-eyed boy who resembled all the Townsend men working on a neighboring farm. Robert took responsibility for the boy's education and welfare. Robert Townsend, known during the war as Culper Junior, died on March 7, 1838 at the age of eighty-four."

"So they never found the treasure?" Aiden asked Mr. Townsend.

"No, and I don't believe there is one, or it would have been found by now," he stated matter-of-factly.

Dealer saw the disappointment cloud Aiden's face. He had been excited about finding the letter in his family Bible and the possibility of discovering hidden treasure. She gently patted his hand as he got to his feet and headed for the door. "What do you propose we do now, Dealer?" he asked.

"I propose," she said with an exasperating smile, "that we don't give up."

Chapter 18

THE FRIENDS MET THE next day at Country Corners Restaurant after school for one of their usual diner experiences of hamburgers and French fries and further discussion about the mystery that seemed to be consuming them.

"Elizabeth hasn't shown up for work yet so we're a little short-handed today, kids," Betty told them. Clearly she was exasperated. "Here's some French fries you can all share until I get caught up on my tables. I'll be back for your order in a minute."

There was no argument from Aiden, who dived in like he hadn't eaten for a week. With the fry still hanging out his mouth, he said, "I heard about Elizabeth; didn't she have some sort of run-in with Simcoe? The rumor is that she helped a prisoner who was arrested for tax evasion escape from the county jail. Just so happens that Simcoe made a citizen's arrest and had her put behind bars for a day or two. Everyone was happy that she had helped the guy, but there was no proof that she did so they had to release her. Do you think her not being here has something to do with that?"

"Who knows? I think I remember reading something about it in the paper. She's probably just late. Speaking of missing, has anyone seen Nathan lately?" Dex asked as he heaved a deep, annoyed sigh.

"I haven't seen or heard from him. I have no idea where he is," Dealer replied, hesitation in her voice. "He wasn't in school again today. I think that trip underground really did a number on him. That coupled with Ms. Arnold's cruel tactics. Speaking of tactics, I need to be upfront with you guys and tell you that I went back down under the school yesterday."

"You did what?! What would make you do a stupid thing like that, especially by yourself? Are you trying to get yourself killed?" Dex was clearly angry.

"You're right," Dealer responded. "It was a totally dumb thing to do, but I felt compelled to check it out again, and you weren't available for consultation. That's all."

"Did you encounter the ghoul of Melville?" Aiden asked with a slight laugh, not taking the situation nearly as seriously as Dex.

"Yeah, I did. There's definitely something going on down there. I heard that scream again, and it scared the crap out of me. I got out of there before I had a chance to see more than Ms. Arnold looking over sheets of microfiche."

"Don't ever do that again, Dealer!" demanded Dex. "You took too much of a risk. What if she saw you? What if Simcoe was there, and the two of them nabbed you? You have no idea of what they are capable of! What you did was so stupid I can't even think straight!"

The heated discussion got Betty's attention. "You kids okay over there? I know I'm behind, but don't get your panties in a wad. I'm coming! I'm coming!"

With that, she moved between the tables and stood at attention at Dex's elbow. "What can I get you folks?"

With burgers ordered and Betty out of ear shot, they picked up their conversation. "You're right, Dex. I'm sorry. What I did was dumb, and I did get the shit scared out of me. I think we need to go back, though. I think there's someone down there who needs help."

"It's more like someone who is still down there needs our help. I don't think Nathan ever called the police," Riley cut in.

"We're safer in numbers. We'll take a real flashlight next time. Before we decide when to go, let's try to decipher this map I found in the trunk first."

"We're not going back down there, Dealer!" Dex said adamantly.

Ignoring him, she pushed the basket of fries to the edge of the table and laid the treasure map in the center. "After looking at this map, I think there may be a better way to get to Tea Island via the tunnels under the school."

"A map? What map? You never said anything about finding a treasure map!" Aiden stammered, enthusiasm rising in his voice.

"With all the excitement I must have forgotten," Dealer assured him pleasantly. "And I don't know if it's a treasure map. I found it in the lining of Robert and Lydia's trunk."

"Are you kidding me? I should fire you for holding back important information and keeping us all in the dark, but then it's your trunk and your map, huh?!" Aiden teased.

"Well, I'll see what I can do about the timing of my deliveries — just for you!"

"Good! Maybe it's the clue we've been waiting for. I can't wait to see where this takes us."

"Nowhere. It's not taking us anywhere," Dex said with enough firmness that his friends became instantly withdrawn. They finished their burgers in silence.

Chapter 19

ON HER WAY TO the bus stop early the next morning, Dealer decided to take the route by Lake George. The suitcase she had seen was still on the shoreline. The small laps of water splashed up on the bank, wrapping the suitcase in wetness. She had a few minutes so she decided to satisfy her curiosity.

She dumped her backpack by a spice bush and kicked off her shoes. The case was heavy, waterlogged from being half submerged in the lake. She dragged it toward her, realizing she hadn't expected it to be so difficult to move. The latch had become somewhat rusted, and she broke a fingernail trying to lift up its lip. She found a nearby rock and hit the metal as hard as she could. The lid popped open.

Dealer started screaming uncontrollably. The high-pitched piercing cry bounced off the water and tumbled through the air. Neighbors heard her and came running, fear filling the atmosphere. There, staring back at her were the sad, empty eyes of Nathan, his face covered in blood and sealife. Beside his body was his backpack with the sticker that Mrs. Arnold had placed on it. She blacked out.

- - - - - - - - - - - - - -

Dealer's first memory afterwards was Dex's distraught gaze peering at her. He was holding her hand. It was then she realized she was in a hospital bed, an IV taped to her arm. Sobs began to rack her body. "Please tell me it was my imagination, that it wasn't Nathan in that suitcase, just some creepy look-alike doll, and he's actually okay!"

"I'm sorry, Dealer," Dex responded quietly. "I wish I could tell you that, but it was Nathan. He's dead. The whole town's in an uproar. The cops are already canvasing the area and conducting a house-to-house investigation in hopes of apprehending his killer right away."

Holding back further tears, Dealer whispered, "We know who killed him, Dex."

"You may be right, but there's no proof," he responded sadly.

"Simcoe and Ms. Arnold did it! I know they did! They were following us the other night when Nathan left for home. Riley and Aiden followed him only part way." Dealer was on the verge of hysteria.

"Get control of yourself, Dealer," Dex urged. "What reason did either or both of them have to kill Nathan? If people hear you making those kinds of accusations, they're going to think you're paranoid and have lost your mind. It's best for now to keep quiet. We'll find the treasure, Dealer; let the police find Nathan's killer."

"What if they try to kill us, too," she murmured, suddenly afraid.

"We'll stick together like always," he said, grabbing her hand in his.

His touch always sent electric pulses through her body, and his concern for her touched her deeply. "Dex…" The door to her hospital room opened, and in walked their friends, their hearts clearly heavy with the news of Nathan's death.

Elsea gave her a one-sided smile, doing her best not to focus on the tragedy. She shoved a thin booklet toward Dealer.

"What's this?" she asked, the mysterious episodes in their lives pulling her thoughts in another direction.

"It's a series of diary entries written by my great-aunt who cared for an old Yankee soldier before he died."

"Where did you find it?"

"Like yours, our farmhouses are all old — antiques actually," Elsea said with a hint of lightheartedness. "Riley and I decided to start with her basement first. We found old pictures, and that got Riley all excited!"

Riley felt a little embarrassed about getting excited over old pictures. She shook her head in denial. "Did not! Let me tell the rest because you're going to mess it up, Elsea!"

"Thanks a lot!" Elsea said sarcastically. In fact, she seemed relieved that Riley was going to do the talking.

"We started rummaging through boxes filled with all sorts of memorabilia — vintage dresses, old pictures, and an old Bible."

"It was Riley's great-great so on and so forth aunt's Bible," Elsea interrupted.

Riley put her hand on Elsea's. "Let me tell it. There was a diary hidden between its pages. There are quite a few entries written about an old man she cared for at a nursing home for veterans. He talked about the war and how he was Nathan Hale's servant."

"You're kidding," Dealer said as she tried to lift herself up onto her elbows. "That's really interesting because my dad found an old book that talks about a nurse helping an old man in a retirement home. Was there any mention of Abercrombie's gold in your aunt's diary?"

"He knew about it, but there is no mention of anyone finding it," Riley went on. "They did try, though. He also spoke about an underground tunnel that the Patriots hid in to ambush the Redcoats."

"Was the tunnel or the men ever discovered?" Dealer probed further.

"They came really close one day. There was a tough old lady named Nancy Hart. She had one heck of a temper, and the six-foot tall woman was fearless. She lived near where the school is located today and hid patriots in some man-made tunnels located there that were patterned after a Native American labyrinth."

Dealer suddenly forgot where she was and why she was there. "You know, you may just be onto something, Riley! I think maybe we were in those tunnels."

"The diary doesn't tell us, but it does say that one of the British soldiers shot Nancy's prized turkey and ordered her to cook it. The last thing she probably wanted to do was feed those lobster backs! She may have been one mean mother, but she was smart. She quietly fed them and served them lots of wine. Then Ms. Hart instructed her daughter to retrieve the conch shell that she kept in a nearby tree stump and to blow into it to alert the men in hiding that the British were in the cabin, and they should make their escape. While the drunken British soldiers were sprawled out in a stupor, she gathered up all their guns. When they awoke, she held them at gunpoint and waited for the villagers to capture them and haul them off to prison."

"It seems logical that the men would have made their escape from those tunnels. I think that should be our next move — look for those tunnels," Elsea stated emphatically.

Dex regarded the group critically. "How do we know the tunnels under the school are those tunnels, and if they are, how do we know they are safe?"

"I'm with Elsea," Aiden finally said. "We won't know anything unless we check it out. Everything seems to point to that red door that leads to the basement of the school, and I say we go back there."

Dex moved uneasily but had no better suggestion. "Okay. Is there more you want to tell us, or did you cover everything?"

"Yes, there's more," Riley answered. "There may be additional clues; maybe it's not in a tunnel."

A nurse interrupted when she came in. "The doctor has cleared your release, young lady. Your dad will be here to pick you up in a few minutes. I'm going to ask your friends to step out into the waiting room while I unhook you from all these gadgets and help you get dressed."

- - - - - - - - - - - - - -

For a few minutes a dark cloud hung over the kitchen table at the Townsend home. A friend had been lost, and there were no words to express a single thought regarding Nathan's senseless murder.

Dealer's dad sat a box of tissues in the middle of the table, and five hands grabbed it at the same time. That was just enough to remind them that they were a connected team as a muffled giggle slipped through Riley's lips.

"Go ahead and read some of those diary pages, Elsea, and let's see if we can learn anything," Dealer said.

"Okay. Here goes. Agent 355's great niece, Daisy Brewster, was a nurse who attended to the veterans of the American Revolution. This is her diary, and it has tons of information about the war and its corresponding spies, as told by Asher Wright, a member of the Culper Spy Ring."

For the next hour Elsea read numerous pages from the diary. Finally she finished reading. It was as if they had all been holding their breath because the room filled with the sound of exhaling air when she stopped.

Dealer's dad had joined them, a calm but troubled look upon his face, while Elsea read from the diary. "This sounds a lot like the stories my mom told me about my great aunt," he said. "She mentioned a treasure map, but she didn't think anything of it, believing that the loot had been dug up long ago."

None of the friends were so sure. Dealer wondered if the map she had found in the attic trunk was the same map that Asher spoke of. She wondered if Nathan had mentioned the tunnels to the wrong person. She wondered what they were missing.

"Let's go outside," she said.

Chapter 20

THE FRESHLY-MOWN GRASS in the front yard offered a therapeutic reprieve. Chewing on a piece of clover somehow seemed to improve the thinking process. "You know," Elsea continued, "I just remembered my cousin Orris told me about a cave he and his sister Blanche discovered by Lake George. They stumbled upon a sink hole hidden in a thick woody area that was disguised by an undergrowth of vines and flowers. Curiosity got the best of him, and he let himself down into the hole just enough to see that the opening extended to an unknown depth. He saw Yankee muskets and other military odds and ends strewn about. Apparently there were beautiful stalactites and stalagmites, too.

"I remember when I was little, Mom and Dad talked about a haunted cave, but I thought it was a myth they were repeating. Somebody reported moaning sounds, and a party of men found the cave and ventured in to investigate it and were never seen again. No one has gone down there and survived. Supposedly it's plagued with treacherous water, maybe quicksand, and muddy embankments. That's the legend anyway. Maybe there's some truth to it after all."

"Anybody who believes that stuff needs a psychiatrist!" Aiden exclaimed.

"Maybe, maybe not," Dealer said. "Irrational things are often found to be rational, and where's there's smoke, there's fire. I wouldn't write off those tunnels or caves just yet. I mean we did find a house of sorts under Melville High."

"Now that I've thought it through, me neither," Dex agreed. "It's not going to be a scenic drive, but we should take it just the same."

- - - - - - - - - - - - - - -

Dealer was afraid; she was very afraid. Frightful memories of her last trip to the school's basement still remained close at hand. But even knowing what they knew, they were drawn to the unknown and determined to find some answers. If it was there, it was important to find the cave entrance that Asher Wright had spoken of to Daisy. For some reason the sleuths were convinced that it was, although it had been hidden for at least 200 years.

By nightfall the five of them had secretly left their homes to meet at the famous rock monument. The whole time Dealer was sneaking down the back door stairs, she felt guilty about not telling her dad, but she knew there was no way he would approve. She hoped she wasn't jeopardizing the closeness and trust they had finally gained after so many months of sorrow and mistrust. It was a chance she was willing to take. This was vitally important.

Quietly she shut the screen door. The amber in her necklace began to glow. She didn't remember it glowing quite so brightly before. She knew for a certainty *The Lady* was beside her, guiding her every move. For some strange reason Dealer felt she would protect her; at least she hoped so.

Dealer found herself feeling vulnerable. Talking was different from doing, and she suddenly remembered just how afraid she was. She knew at that moment she should turn around and go back into the house. But how could she? She was already committed.

In the distance she saw her friends congregated behind the statue, waiting impatiently for her. She had taken longer than was necessary, stopping every so often to listen to the night.

They nodded to one another and without saying a word, headed to the rocks where the underground cave led to the old house. Getting inside was the easy part; getting out was what Dealer feared the most.

Dex seemed to be in tune with her, and to assuage some of her fear, he took her hand as they headed toward their destination. The closer they got to the red door, the harder she squeezed his hand. She was scared, and it struck her that the fact that the door was painted red unnerved her even more.

When Dex unlocked the door, Dealer felt a slight wisp of wind pass by her, and she could only hope it was *The Lady* and that she approved of what they were doing.

Dealer was sure everyone felt the same as she did — that she felt like she had lead boots on instead of tennis shoes. They moved so slowly down the stairs they got in each other's way, and somebody stepped on her foot. Then she realized she had stepped on her own foot, and fear gripped her even harder.

The coast seemed to be clear. In hushed silence they moved around the columns and skirted past the parlor toward the back where Dealer had heard a woman scream the visit before. The space was huge, and it was difficult to tell where the walls ended. "Is there anybody behind that gate?" Elsea whispered so softly they barely heard her.

The light was so dim Dealer had to strain to see, but she couldn't make out anything definitive. The suspended bulb was not switched on so it was difficult to make out anything. A strange odor hung in the air. All of them were holding hands as Dex gingerly led them toward the bars.

Peering through them, they realized a woman was strapped to a table, probably the same woman they had seen before. She wasn't a ghost; she was a real live person. She had dark brown, wavy hair, and she looked familiar. Even in the faint light they could see that her eyes were filled with terror.

"That's the waitress from the diner," Dex managed to say. The rest of his friends were unable to speak.

Finally Aiden managed to say something. "It's Elizabeth Burgin."

Dex gripped the bars and began lightly shaking them. "Hold on a second." He rummaged in his pocket for his special tools. His hands shook so badly he fumbled at the lock without success. Dealer quietly took them from him and attempted to pick the lock like she had seen Dex do it. Just when Dex was ready to try again, the tumbler fell into place and disengaged the mechanism with a click.

When she realized her visitors were not Simcoe and Ms. Arnold, Elizabeth began to cry. "I ... I did...n't believe anyone would fi...fi...find me," she stammered, her body shaking uncontrollably.

"Shhh, it's okay," Dex soothed. "We have to be as quiet as possible. You're safe now; we're here, and we'll help you."

"Simcoe kidnapped me! He's a monster! You've got to get me out of here!" Hysteria was consuming her, and she fought as Dealer held her hand over Elizabeth's mouth.

"We know, but you've got to be quiet before you get us all killed," Dealer insisted. Red needle marks mottled the length of her arms, and a deeper fear settled into Dealer's bones. They were definitely dealing with monsters.

Elizabeth attempted to gain her composure. "I'm not an addict. Simcoe did this to me. They are all undead, and they were drinking my blood. Please, please hurry! Get me out of here," she managed to say, the recollection causing her to shake again.

"We know he did." Aiden did his best to comfort her, and he, too, felt a sense of dread and was aware of the potential danger that could assault them at any moment.

"Then you believe me?"

"We all believe you. We are well aware of what he's capable of," Dex said.

"Then get me out of here! He's here; I feel it. He's going to hurt me again. Please ... Please ..." Elizabeth pleaded.

She was frantic. They were all frantic. None of them knew how to withdraw a needle from a vein, but Dex thought to apply pressure at its tip and pull it straight out. When he did, Elizabeth's blood began squirting everywhere. Riley managed a partial scream before she crumpled to the floor.

Dealer quickly put her finger over the needle hole and then replaced her finger with Elizabeth's. "Don't let go," she whispered, "and be very quiet!" Nobody said a word. Elsea and Dex worked at loosening the straps. Minutes felt like hours. The fear Dealer felt in the pit of her stomach was almost too much. Her skin began to prickle, and she had a sense of uncanny forces surrounding them. Many sufferings were buried in this underground structure, and they had to get out ... before it was too late.

Riley regained consciousness, and they slowly sat her up so she could get her bearings. "I'm fine now," she said reassuringly. "I'm not good with blood, and I'm definitely not good with squirting blood. Is Elizabeth all right?"

"She's going to be, but we've got to get moving." Instinctively they all followed Dex as he left the cage. Dealer grabbed Elizabeth's free hand, and they edged further along the back wall.

"Where are you going? We have to get out of this house," Elizabeth wailed, her shrill voice rising.

"Calm down, Elizabeth," Dealer said quietly. "I know it's easy for me to say because I haven't been through what you've been through, but you've got to trust us. If Simcoe is the monster we all believe him to be, our best bet is to find another way out. If he's here, we could be walking right into him. I'm not prepared to do that. Are you?"

"N---noooo. But how do we find another way out?"

"We think there is a series of underground tunnels here," Dex said quietly. "We suspect he doesn't know about them."

"Well, before he learns, can we get out of here?" Elsea whispered.

Dealer didn't tell them, but she felt *The Lady* urge her in the direction they should go. "Let's use some logic and follow this wall," she suggested. "It looks like it could be part of a corridor, but it won't be obvious."

"We have to be careful," Aiden pointed out. "The light is terrible down here, and anything built 200 years ago is going to be in serious disrepair. It could be even more dangerous than Simcoe. Maybe we should take our chances and go out the way we came in."

Suddenly a maniacal and terrifying scream pierced the air. They stopped dead in their tracks. There was a moment of intense startled silence, then Elsea said, "I don't think we can go back. I think Simcoe and Arnold found Elizabeth missing. We've got to find another way out of here if we're going to survive."

Dealer knew she was right, but she felt confused and indecisive. Most of all she wanted to run, to get away from those hideous screams.

Dex made the decision for all of them. "We're going to follow the damp air and see if we can find those tunnels. If we don't, at least we will be hidden enough to be safe for a while. Let's go." He was calm, but he was clearly unsettled about the circumstances.

Slowly they made their way along the wall, looking for any sign of something different and unusual that might lead them to safety. More moaning and screaming reached the building where they were clustered, and in unison they all shuffled faster along the wall. Dex took Dealer's hand, and she followed closely behind, Elizabeth in tow. It was difficult to see, but Dealer didn't have to see faces to know how frightened they all were.

Progress seemed painstakingly slow. Quiet now permeated the air, making them even more afraid that someone would hear them so they hardly moved at all. Dealer prayed they were not traveling into the pits of Hell. She could feel water trickling down the walls and noticed the concrete floor had ended. They were now walking in soft mud. Tennis shoes squeaked and made squishy sounds, and a couple of times she fell, but Dex and Dealer never let go of Elizabeth. Most certainly they were all covered in mud, but it was better than what they had left behind.

All the tales and superstitions Elsea had told them vanished when they miraculously came upon an enormous cave. Soft light came from somewhere unknown, and they saw that they were surrounded with rock pinnacles, cliffs, and gorges. A makeshift sign that read "King's Palace" had been hung on the wall, and Dealer wondered if one of the Patriots had put it there as a joke.

The chamber was so vast that she would have sworn that it could easily accommodate forty Boeing 747 airplanes. Its size took her breath away.

Their entrance into the cavern disturbed the birds, and droves of them began to chatter and reprimand the group noisily. "Those look like hornbills," Elsea said. "If there are birds, surely there is an exit."

There has to be, Dealer thought to herself.

Somehow the chamber gave them a small sense of comfort so they began to separate and put a little distance between each other as they walked on. "Gross," Dealer said almost too loudly and clearly disgusted as she scraped the sole of her shoe onto a protruding rock on the floor. "Those may be hornbills, but over here there's a huge population of bats and all the filth that goes with them! Look at that mound of guano. It's almost as high as the ceiling."

"Gross is right." Dex gave a hollow laugh.

"Could we take a rest just for a little bit?" Riley asked. The adrenalin rush had lasted too long, and she was beginning to feel overly tired.

"Sure, we can probably do that. We need to calm our nerves anyway," Aiden agreed. Riley clearly appeared relieved.

"Quite frankly I can tell you I'm a little worried," Dex admitted. "The good news is I can feel some fresh air so let's take a load off for a few minutes before we move on and see what Dealer's got in that backpack of hers. It's always full of snacks!" He tried his best to be cheerful as he playfully grabbed at her backpack.

Sure enough Dealer had leftovers. There was some water, cookies, a half-eaten peanut butter sandwich, and gummy bears.

"How are you feeling, Elizabeth? Tell us about yourself," Dealer prompted in an attempt to break the heavy silence and give her a brief moment to calm the tension that was building up inside of her.

At first, she couldn't find words to speak. Then she seemed to resign herself to the situation and the need to express. Her voice rang hollow with memories. "When I was younger, I worked as a nurse during the Afghanistan war for the Red Cross. I smuggled food to the American prisoners and treated their wounds and comforted them as best I could. One day one of the Afghan soldiers discovered what I was doing and had me imprisoned. One of the other guards was sympathetic toward me and helped me escape and smuggled me out of Afghanistan. I found my way back to a base camp. From there I was flown back to the United States where I recovered in a hospital. When I was well enough, I came back to Setauket to be with my family. They are struggling financially and on the verge of losing their farm so I took the waitressing job at Country Corners to help with the mortgage. That's Elizabeth Burgin in a nutshell."

"But why did Simcoe kidnap you and put you in this place?" Aiden asked incredulously.

Slim shoulders drooped further. "I was an easy target for blood. I was locking up after working the late shift, and someone grabbed me from behind and covered my nose with a handkerchief. That's the last thing I remember until they brought me to this dungeon. They have been drawing my blood on a regular basis, and had you not saved me, I surely would have died. Until I saw you, Dealer, I thought I was dead. I'm sure no one has any idea where I am, and my parents are so old they may not even know I'm missing. Thank God for you kids! You saved my life."

None of the teens knew what to say. Could this all be for real? "We need to get going," Dex said as he dusted off his pants and held out his hand to Dealer. "It won't be long before our parents will realize we aren't where we're supposed to be. It's also possible Simcoe and Ms. Arnold will come looking for us; we present a huge threat to them and whatever it is they are up to. We have to find a way out of here."

They nodded their heads in agreement. The damp floor became scattered with moss-covered rocks as they moved further through the cave, and then they heard the sound of moving water. "We need to be careful here," Dex instructed. "It's super slippery. Running water means there's a way out."

About 50 yards ahead they reached their destination. Dex spoke positively, "The buck stops here I'm afraid. This appears to be an underground river. Underneath its surface is probably the only way out. There's no way to know without checking it out. We have to either turn back, or one of us is going to have to swim down and see if there is an adjacent cavern where we can resurface and escape."

Dealer smiled faintly, knowing he was right. "Well, we can't go back. At least I'm too scared to chance it. Simcoe is sure to have found Elizabeth gone by now."

Aiden stiffened as he leaned slightly over the edge. "Want me to go first?"

"I'm the oldest and probably the strongest so thanks, but no. I think I should be the one to go," Dex said.

Dealer was terrified for Dex. What was under the water? How far would he have to swim? What if he could not make it? But Dex was the only hope they had. "You'll need to strip down to your underwear. Less drag will make it easier for you to swim, especially if there are currents."

"Yeah, I know. This is my debut so suck it up, boys and girls, and let me hear your applause!" Dex was scared, and all of them understood his desperation in masking it. They chuckled and lightly applauded as he began to take off his clothes.

"Mickey Mouse boxers? Are you kidding me?!" Riley couldn't help but rib her friend.

"Well, it's better than none at all so count your blessings!"

"Wait, Dex. I have some twine in my backpack. For the first time in my life I'm thanking the school for requiring art classes! They serve a purpose after all! When you find a way out, tug on it so we know you're okay." It was feeble. It was weak. But it was the best Dealer could do.

"That's a great idea! We can use it to help me guide you to where you need to swim once I find a way out." Dealer tied the twine around his ankle and squeezed his leg for luck. A shiver went through her as he bowed and dived into the freezing water.

As if they had just lost their lifeline, the friends stared wide-eyed at each other. How were they going to get out alive?

- - - - - - - - - - - - - -

The underground canyon turned northwest before it began to get smaller. Dex held his breath and pushed on as hard as he dared, conserving the breath in his lungs as long as he could. Murky water clouded his vision, but vaguely he could see some light ahead piercing through the water. His legs began to tire, and his lungs began to burn; surely he was almost there.

Something in his gut made him swim on instead of turning back. Panic almost seized him when he realized at this point there really was no going back. He was becoming lightheaded. He reached out with his hands and grabbed onto a ledge where the sun's rays were bleeding through.

Exhaustion seized him; he was barely able to pull himself onto the rock shelf where there was a pocket of air and a huge underground chamber. His chest pounded, and he struggled to catch his breath. The trek had been a close call. He surveyed his surroundings and saw that there were hundreds of artifacts and quite a few skeletons. He wondered for a moment if they were part of Abercrombie's crew. Or maybe they are explorers like me looking for missing treasure, he thought. Either way, I'm frickin cold and too tired to swim back to my friends.

Dex leaned over and pulled the twine hard twice, letting his friends know he was okay. He was worried that they might not make it if they tried following him, but there was no way to let them know. They hadn't discussed what to do once he reached a safe place.

Chapter 21

TIME DRAGGED ON, AND Dealer was losing hope. They all were. The tug took Dealer by surprise. She was elated. Dex had made it safely to somewhere. She moved uneasily and looked down at the twine wrapped around her ankle. "Thank God! He's safe, or at least we think he is. Who's going to follow him?"

"I'm not a strong swimmer, and I have no energy with the blood loss I've sustained over the last few days. I'll have to wait here because there's no going back," Elizabeth stated somberly.

"Don't feel bad," Elsea said. "I would only drag you guys down as well. I'm a lousy swimmer so I'll stay and hold the twine for anyone who is able to attempt the swim."

"I guess that leaves the three of us. Are we ready to go?"

"I'm as ready as I'll ever be," Aiden said. He seemed pretty sure of himself; he was a strong swimmer.

"I'm going, Dealer," Riley replied with a tinge of uncertainty.

"Let's go then so we don't leave Dex waiting too long." The three stripped down as much as they could without being embarrassed and took three big breaths. Aiden and Riley dove right in, each holding the life line that connected them to Dex on one end and Elsea on the other. Dealer hesitated. Slowly she inched her way into the water until she was chest high.

"Are you okay?" Elsea asked.

"I'll be fine." Dealer smiled with misplaced confidence and ducked under the water.

Chapter 22

DEALER COULD BARELY SEE Riley's feet kicking in the water just ahead so she swam faster so she could to get to the line. Just when they thought their lungs would burst, a small ray of light appeared. Dealer felt the twine veer off to the right.

Aiden spotted a hand coming down into the water and with great relief took Dex's outstretched fingers as his friend quickly pulled him out of the water. Riley and Dealer followed, but Dealer was so cold and exhausted she couldn't lift herself up. Dex and Aiden desperately yanked her arm in unison to get her out of the water. She flopped out on the rock floor, attempting to catch her breath.

The cave was cold, but the sunlight filtering through a small hole at the top of the roof provided a measure of heat. They shivered together, their arms wrapped around their bodies. It was a miracle they had made it, and they knew it.

While he had been waiting for them, Dex had spotted another opening in a side wall. He pointed at it anxiously.

"Oh, my God! Are we going to have to go through that now?" Riley's tone was disbelieving. "With the few clothes we have on, we're sure to be scraped raw. Talk about leaving a blood trail!"

"Well, these aren't normal circumstances, Riley; that's for sure. We're suffering the consequences over which we have no control," Dex returned, doing his best to speak lightly of the situation. "It's okay if you don't want to squeeze through. I think we need someone here to hold the twine so we can have another anchor in this voyage. That way if Elizabeth or Elsea tug, you can tug back. It might give them some comfort. Then again, it might make them think we haven't found a way out."

"I'm willing and able, but seriously… Can I take a moment to breathe before we head out again?" Dealer begged.

"Not a problem. Here, you hold the rope for a minute. I'm going to scout ahead. Whenever you're ready, give the lead to Riley. Then you and Aiden follow me."

"You guys have to be careful," Riley advised. "I heard this morning that it is supposed to rain sometime this afternoon. I've read in books that large underground caves like this one can flood quickly if it rains so we have just a few hours."

"You better hope and pray we get through here in time, or we're all dead. So hurry up," Aiden pushed.

After Riley's speech, Dex didn't have to be coaxed, and he was gone.

Dealer caught her breath and stood up. "Time's a-wastin', and I'm not getting any younger. Let's go, Aiden."

As soon as Riley realized she was going to be all by herself, she chickened out. "I'm coming, too." She found a large heavy rock and tied the twine around it. "That should do it. Let's go."

It took some maneuvering to get through the opening, and success didn't come without casualties. All three had road rash on their arms, legs, and backs, but fear lodged and loomed in their memories, and for the moment they hardly noticed.

Once through, a magical scene bombarded their senses. Dealer was amazed at the incredible ecosystem that had developed in the cave. A sprawling garden of various plant and rock life lay before them. Beautiful pink and vivid blue flowers were jutting out of rocks. Tiny cups of purple clung to a spot on the wall, their tendrils clinging to small fragments of rock. Crystals in the minerals shone in the faint sunlight. Pebbles worn smooth by the flow of water gathered in heaps. A beautiful noise of water tinkling reminded Dealer of wind chimes playing in the soft breeze.

With her mind on the beauty that surrounded her, Dealer didn't notice the pools of blood collecting on her hands and legs. She did notice Aiden's, though. "This trek is taking a toll on our bodies," she commented as she studied the trail of blood left behind them. "No crumbs for the birds here," she said jokingly. "Just a path of drips and splatters."

"I hate to say 'I told you so,' but I did," Riley slipped in.

"My knees, hands, and everything else are killing me," Aiden responded. "I hope there is a . . . ouch!"

"What happened?"

"I was busy looking back at you, Riley, and hit my head on this low overhang of rock. Now my head's a bloody mess, too!"

"Sorry." Her sympathy fell on deaf ears.

"Wait! I see Dex up ahead. Good grief, there is a another huge cavern. It's even bigger than the one we left Elsea and Elizabeth in."

"Get going! I want to see!"

As Aiden moved aside, Dealer took a look into the cave. Its near darkness seemed to envelope her in a never-ending fortress of mystic wonder. She wiggled inside, breathing in the stale, humid air as she used the rough cave wall to guide her through it. She could hear a soft dripping noise as dew slid off the rocks. Drip, drip, drip, like a heartbeat. Dim light vaguely lit spires of rock that hung from the ceiling; others stood erect on the floor. A soft squeak alerted her to the presence of either rats or bats. The chilly draft and the thought of creepy miscreants sent shivers down her spine. As if sensing her need for warmth, the amber rock that lay on her chest heated up and spread a soft glow in front of her.

They joined Dex and took in the vast array of the enormous room. "Who would have ever thought?" he said, expressing the awe they all felt. Hesitantly they moved in unison along the murky aisles further into the cave. They walked wearily forward. Dealer felt disorientated and exhausted as her eyes adjusted to the darkness. Her feet felt like suction cups in the wet mud on the cave floor. It was fairly warm, but she was freezing.

Presently they came to a place where a little stream of water trickled over a ledge, carrying the same limestone sediment that they had seen in the first cavern. It had, through the slow-dragging ages, formed a laced and ruffled Niagara-type falls in gleaming imperishable stones. Just as one would have imagined it, a treasure chest with coins laying all around it sat half buried in dust behind the stone waterfall. Dex squeezed Dealer's hand as the three of them stood there and wordlessly gazed at it.

Right behind the treasure chest a steep stairway had been carved between the narrow walls. All at once realities culminated, and they felt the exhilaration of finding the treasure and another red door. This wasn't a Robert Louis Stevenson story; it was the real thing.

Dealer suddenly knew they weren't alone; the amber in her necklace had warned her. She subconsciously ignored it. For a moment, she thought she heard something, but the echo within the cave made it impossible to tell where the sound was coming from. Every move they made disturbed the bats and cave rats, and the cacophony of a thousand flapping wings drown out all other noise.

Dealer almost jumped out of her skin when an outstretched hand grabbed hers. It was Mr. Simcoe. An inaudible scream hung in her throat, and she froze.

Chapter 23

"DID YOU KNOW THAT this cavern is called 'The Chamber of the Lost Child?' Simcoe asked as he slithered around them. "A child — it is not recorded who or when — found his way into this cave and got lost in it. It was a very rainy day, and as you probably know, when it rains, the caves and tunnels flood. He must have wandered for many hours, possibly days, inside this incredible labyrinth of chambers without ever finding his way out. His skeleton, covered with stalagmitic material, was found intact; actually I found it just a few hours ago. He must have laid here for decades amongst the treasure chest of gold that I see you've found."

"How did you get here?" Dealer managed to ask harshly. "You didn't follow us because you're perfectly dry."

"There's another entrance on Tea Island where you expected the gold to be hidden. I chose that route."

"What in the hell are you?" Dex screamed, trying to mask his terror with bravery.

Simcoe just smiled and held out his arm; a bat fluttered down and rested on it. "I died in the Revolutionary War," he grinned with an eerie smile. "I had the pleasure of being unearthed one day by men who were excavating the site where the extension of the high school is built. They made the mistake of messing with my skeleton. The rest is history. I don't think I've ever witnessed such fright. It pleased me greatly to feed on their terrorized bodies. Naturally I disposed of them. There were no tales to be told of their discovery."

"I remembered reading about their disappearance in the paper. It's still an unsolved mystery," Aiden sputtered.

"Yes, yes, I supposed it is at that. There are soon to be more unsolved mysteries," Simcoe informed them with a freaky grin.

"Elizabeth was right. You are a monster!" Riley was in a state of shock.

"Now that you have us cornered, what are you going to do to us?" Dex could barely speak, fear engulfing his sense of reason.

Simcoe spread his hands blandly. "It's simple really. Dealer's family has something I want, and if she gives it to me, you will all go free, and you can save your homes and families from me and my friends," he said looking up at all the bats hovering above them.

"What does my family have that you could possibly want?" she asked, her face tightening into a mask of anger.

"I want the necklace. I want *The Lady*. We have some unfinished business, she and I. She is a traitor, and for that she will pay dearly. She's the one who told Tallmadge where I was hiding," Simcoe growled. "They lined me up against a wall and shot me while she stood watching. I loved her! She will pay for what she did to me!" he cried passionately, his fists clenched by his sides. "Before I died I cast a spell on her amulet. I will take her to hell with me . . . her and her lover Robert and feed on their souls for eternity!"

The amber burned Dealer's skin, and she screamed. Clearly *The Lady* didn't want the amulet to get in Simcoe's possession. She wanted them to escape but how? Dealer looked for a place to run, but they were trapped.

Simcoe's voice dropped to a whisper. "You're not thinking of running away, are you? There is no escape from me! Where is the amber amulet?" His eyes glared, and he began to tremble. Bony fingers edged their way toward Dealer.

"Let go of her arm!" Dex yelled.

"Like there's anything you can do! You don't frighten me, boy!" Simcoe cackled unpleasantly. "You'd do best to convince your little lady friend here to tell me where the necklace is and to tell me quickly! I haven't forgotten how to eliminate bodies."

Maybe there was a way to buy some time. Simcoe did not know where the necklace was. Dealer wasn't going to give it to this freak. Suddenly a bat swooped down so close she had to duck for fear it would hit her. All eyes were on Dealer.

"I don't know where it is, but if you let us go, I can look for it…" Dealer's legs were shaking with fear.

"You run along then," Simcoe agreed, pleased with the result of his presence. "Go get the amulet, and when I have it in my hands, you and your friends can go."

She had hoped for a different answer, one that would allow her to stall further. "You can't be trusted! You'll never let us go!"

"Probably not but what choice do you have, Dealer? May I call you that?"

"No!" she shrieked. Instinctively she swung to hit him. It was the opportunity Dex had been waiting for. Simcoe side-stepped her swing, and when he did, Dex tackled him with such furiosity that they landed in a pile of rubble three feet away. Dex was no match for Simcoe as he quickly gained the upper hand. The blood drained from Dex's face as unconsciousness overtook him.

A smug grin spread across Simcoe's face as he rose to his feet.

Chapter 24

FEAR AND DREAD HUNG in the air, and no one moved. It was as if some unknown force held them in place.

Suddenly another man and woman appeared beside Simcoe. She was beautiful with long strawberry blonde hair and naked except for the python that entwined her body. Dealer felt sick.

"May I introduce you to Lilu," Simcoe said, as he moved his hand indifferently. "Or as you know her, Ms. Arnold. The sad gentleman is Robert Townsend; he can't leave this earth while his wife Lydia's soul is trapped in the amulet. That is the spell I put on her."

Dealer wondered briefly if she was in a dream state. Her anger began to rise, and she decided to take a dangerous chance. "Aiden, get your eyes back in your head! These demons aren't going to let us go even if I give them some so-called amulet. I don't even know what it is you're looking for, Simcoe."

"Ahh, but you do. Your great-grandmother was the beautiful woman who held my heart. She betrayed me. I never wanted the stupid treasure! Look, it's been here all this time, and I've done nothing," he said in a low voice.

"You foreclosed on our homes," Aiden suddenly said heatedly.

"Yes, I wanted you to start looking in your basements and attics for old things to sell. I wanted Dealer to find that amulet. Her mother refused me and look what happened to her," Simcoe sneered.

Dealer was sick. "What? You killed my mother?" She felt her knees begin to buckle. Had Aiden not held her up, she would have fallen to the ground.

Simcoe smiled as if the memory brought him joy. "I did have a little something to do with that accident. I thought your dad would sort through her belongings. Instead the idiot took up the bottle. Thank God I still have you."

"You don't have me," she snarled as the witch of Melville High backed the kids up against a wall. There was no place to run as the ghostly woman eyed them hungrily. Dex had slowly regained consciousness and was trying to sit up.

"You can feed on the two boys and young girl but leave Dealer to me," Simcoe spoke to Lilu is a harsh tone. "First, perhaps they can convince her to tell me what it is I want to know!"

There was no one to save them. It wouldn't be long before Elsea and Elizabeth would be discovered, and they would die, too. Sheer terror gripped the air. There seemed to be no prayers anyone could speak.

Abruptly, as if out of nowhere, a flash of blinding light came bursting from Dealer's necklace. *The Lady* stepped out of the light and glared at Simcoe and Lilu.

"Well, there you are, my lovely! I've been waiting for you! I should have known that little brat would have you wrapped around her neck!"

"I was never your lovely, and this has nothing to do with these kids, especially Dealer," Lydia responded. "You're not the only one who has been wronged. I've waited a long time to finally be able to deal with you."

"You are no match for me, Lydia. Even as strong-willed a woman as you are, you can't best me. You haven't got the nerve."

"Assuming has certainly made an ass of you, you dried up piece of dirt." A ball of fire appeared in her hands. She leaned over and blew it toward Simcoe. Expecting the ball to come at him, he quickly dodged it, knocking Dealer to the ground. But the ball didn't move from her hands.

Her ruse had worked. Her breath sought him like a programmed missile and enveloped him in a fog. As soon as Simcoe inhaled Lydia's breath, his body burst into flames. The heat was so intense his dying screams could not escape his mouth. Bats and cave rats by the hundreds, panicked by the blaze, darted and squawked furiously.

Ms. Arnold made an attempt to help him, and instantly she, too, was consumed in flames. The acrid smell of flesh reached Dealer's nostrils, and nausea took over. Her fight mechanism kicked in just in time to save her from throwing up, and she stood up on wobbly legs.

There was nothing but smoldering remains where Simcoe and Ms. Arnold had once stood. The stench must have had the scent of charred meat because the cave rats began creeping out from their hiding places to feed on what was left.

Lydia and Townsend held each other in a long, loving embrace, bridging the gap that time had left. Finally they were free. Speechless, the three teens watched as the two lovers became one in a swirling mist that moved toward Dealer. Then they were gone.

The stench was overwhelming, and there was no time for questions or answers. Yelling for everyone to come, Dex clasped Dealer's hand in his, and the four of them headed for the corridor and the stairs.

They plunged into every new passage they encountered, no thought of the honeycomb that pulled them further from the treasure. The sound of the frenzied bats and rats could no longer be heard, and they slowed to catch their breath.

"I guess we're lost again, aren't we?" Aiden was the first one to speak.

"Yeah, I think we are. Any chance any of you can help us find a way out? We've made so many twists and turns that I have no idea where we are." Dex was dumbfounded with worry.

"I'll do my best," Riley offered. "I have a keen sense of direction, and if we don't get out pretty soon, we're going to be in serious trouble. The rain has probably started, and we won't survive once the water starts flowing."

They retraced their steps as Riley led them back through a corridor. They traveled it in silence for a long way, checking out each opening to see if anything looked familiar. Everything looked untraveled and strange. They watched Riley's face for any sign of encouragement. None came.

"It's going to be all right," Dex told Dealer as he took hold of her arm, but she could tell he felt less and less hopeful as the minutes passed.

Taking a different approach, Riley began to turn off into divergent avenues at random in a desperate attempt to find a way out. Dealer clung to Dex's side, overcome with fear, and tried hard to fight back the tears.

"Listen!" The silence that followed was so deep they were even conscious of their shallow breathing.

Aiden yelled "Hello!" His shout echoed down the empty corridors and died out into a faint sound that resembled a ripple of mocking laughter.

"Stop it!" Riley scolded as she shuddered. The air became colder as the half-naked bodies began to shake. The cave darkened, and all hope seemed to diminish. "Let's sit and rest for a minute and try to reason things through."

No one gave her any resistance as they all huddled close together on a fairly flat rock. Dealer clutched Dex's ice cold hand tightly, and all of her terrors and regrets seemed to pour out from her soul. Turbulent sobs racked her body, and she found she was colder than ever.

"You need to keep it together, Dealer — for everyone's sake," Dex whispered in her ear.

It was then she noticed the blood. "Dex, your neck is bleeding. Let me wipe it off with the tail of my shirt."

"Thanks. Simcoe scratched me good when he and I hit that pile of rocks."

Shifting the attention off herself seemed to be the motivation Dealer needed because she suddenly felt that she could manage the situation. Her back straightened with determination.

As if in a silent, unified decision, they all got up again and began to move forward. Dealer gently held her necklace and prayed that *The Lady* and Robert were still with them. Their situation was dire, but they wandered aimlessly through the passages anyway.

The amber amulet began to glow. *The Lady* was there. Dealer used the light to guide them. When it faded, they turned a different direction. When it glowed strongly, they stayed on their path.

She thought she heard dripping water. Miraculously they ended back where they had started, what was left of the heap that had once been Simcoe and Ms. Arnold still smoldering. A pungent smell of smoke and flesh hung in the air. It was too much for Riley, and she dropped to her knees in exhaustion and horror.

"Shhh! Did you hear that?" Dex held up his hand.

They held their breath. Off in the distance down a corridor she had not noticed before, she thought she heard a muted shout. Instantly Aiden shouted back. They dragged themselves through a rough opening and followed the direction of the sound. The hope of rescue overshadowed the pain of cuts, scratches, and bruises. They stopped and listened again, and again they heard the shouts, only stronger this time.

"I think I hear my dad's voice!" Dealer said excitedly through chattering teeth. "He's coming to save us!"

"I hope he brought some people with him. They're never going to believe what we discovered!" Aiden added. "Funny thing is I haven't thought about that gold since Simcoe made his entrance."

"Me neither," Riley said. "Nor have we thought about Elsea and Elizabeth. I hope they are okay tucked in that cave. Life and death take different priorities, don't they? We were trying to stay alive; I think we may have succeeded."

"You bet your boots we did!" Dex chimed in while holding his neck with his hand. He was elated and overcome with relief.

They were all overwhelmed with happiness. Cautiously they moved around pitfalls, rock formations, and gaping holes. The cave's light was dim, but they managed to make out vague outlines. Had Dex not been paying close attention, though, he would have walked right into a large well hole. They all realized how close they had come to losing him the second time. Fear settled in, and no one had the nerve to jump across the hole's wide expanse. It was just too scary. There was no way to skirt around it so they parked themselves where they stood. Surely rescuers were on their way.

The shouting grew closer, and instantly they were there — Elizabeth, Elsea, Mr. Townsend, three park rangers, a nurse, the fire chief, and the county sheriff. The tears began flooding their faces. They didn't even think to be embarrassed, the four of them standing there in little clothing. They were alive. They were saved. They were safe.

Armed with thick ropes, hoses, first aid kits, and everything else imaginable, the guardian angels just stared at them in disbelief. Even they were speechless.

Finally Elizabeth managed to ask, "Are you guys okay? I've been worried sick about your safety! I found help as soon as I could!"

Aiden finally offered a reply. "We're a little worse for wear, but we're fine. Cold, hungry, exhausted, and damn glad to see you!"

It seemed like the rescue team had scarcely reached them before they were wrapped in warm blankets and hugs. Dealer's head was bowed, and her fingers trembled in Dex's cold hand. He leaned down and kissed her. Endless questions bombarded them, especially regarding Simcoe and Ms. Arnold.

"Their gig's up," Aiden spoke truthfully. "You'll find an ugly scene on the other side of that big hole. We're lucky to be alive."

"Yes, you are," the deputy sheriff remarked. "We'll have to talk later about a couple of good reasons not to take matters into your own hands. But for now, I'll let it rest."

Dealer turned around slowly to see where they had narrowly escaped death. Her eyes searched the penetrating darkness, and there they were — The Lady Lydia and Dealer's great-great-grandfather Robert Townsend, heroes of the American Revolution. They were holding hands. Dealer smiled. They had found each other and were finally at peace. She knew the feeling, and it was good.

They had found the treasure. Simcoe and Ms. Arnold were destroyed. The town and its homes were saved.

Dealer held the warm amulet in the palm of her hand. She did not want to let it go. She felt closer to *The Lady* than she had ever felt toward anyone. The necklace was *The Lady*'s parting gift to her; she would cherish it always.

The town had come together to find the missing teenagers. Dealer's dad had discovered that she was gone and reported it to the police chief. After Nathan's death, no chances had been taken. Volunteers combed the streets, empty buildings, fields, and woods. It was Elizabeth who had ultimately saved them, though. She and Elsea had rallied their strength and found a way to sneak back out of the house without being seen, and she'd gone straight to the authorities, who had been looking in the wrong places.

Tea Island legend took the firefighters rescue team to the sinkhole Elsea's cousin had discovered years before. Prepared with ropes and ladders, they shimmied down into the vast canyon in hopes of finding the missing kids. Excellent headlamps led them straight to where they were clustered together.

- - - - - - - - - - - - - - -

A large funeral was held in Nathan's honor. Dex and Aiden carved a cross to put at the foot of his gravesite. Riley had inscribed it, "In Memory of Nathan, Setauket's hero." They all held hands as the sun went down, and the night sky settled on their shoulders. So much had transpired in the last week, and lifelong friendships had been forged. A new respect for life settled in their hearts as they headed to the diner.

Epilogue

AS DEALER STOOD LOOKING out over the sea off Tea Island, she realized there had been many changes in her life. Each choice she made led her somewhere — sometimes down the right path, other times down the wrong one. But through the love of her friends and family she came out a little older and a little wiser. Dad fixed up their home and paid off the mortgage with some of the reward money the town gave each of the teens for finding the gold. Together they planted crops. There was food on their table and every other table in Setauket, thanks to *The Lady*.

For a moment Dealer's heart sank because she knew she would miss her. Then *The Lady* quickly reminded her that she had never left her side. She was with her even now. The glow of the amber on her chest validated it.

The whole town joined to celebrate the Culper Spy Ring and their descendants. Everyone benefitted from the discovery of the gold on Tea Island. The homes foreclosed on by Simcoe were restored to their rightful owners, and the remainder of the treasure was donated to a museum and a memorial for the unsung heroes of the American Revolution.

Dealer's life had definitely changed since that fateful day when she discovered the hidden trunk, but she could not be happier with where she was. She and Dex had been together ever since his first kiss; maybe they would go to college together now that they could afford it!

Dealer missed her mom terribly, but now that her grandparents lived with them, life was so much better. Grandpa took to helping her dad with the farming, and Grandma made sure meals were cooked, the house taken care of, and the chickens, goats, cows, and horses fed.

Sometimes Dealer and Grandma go up to the attic and draw together and create art projects with her mom's glitter, feathers, and other odds and ends. Sometimes they sift through the letters in the trunk and read them to each other. Sometimes they reflect on the hidden desires of two hearts that were finally one and count their blessings.

This was one of those times. Grandma was dusting a shelf that now held ornate boxes filled with ancient buttons and other memorabilia. The curtains fluttered ever so slightly as a visitor quietly joined them.

- - - - - - - - - - - - - - - -

A lot of fiction surrounds this story; however, it also contains myriad facts about the Revolutionary War, its heroes and heroines, and the roles they played in helping to create America. Many of the truths won't be recorded in your history books, but they exist just the same. I wanted you, the reader, to know that all people — old, young, strong, or weak — played an important role. Even today every one of us can make a difference.

The Culper Spy Ring Code

Robert Tallmadge was a member of the Culper Spy Ring who delivered coded messages on British troop movements through dangerous British lines during the American Revolution. A copy of the code taken from the Mt. Vernon George Washington papers follows. Original spellings have been kept intact. Messages are hidden within the story for you to decipher to find the hidden treasure. Good hunting!

1	a	2	an	37	attone	38	attack
3	all	4	at	39	alarm	40	action
5	and	6	art	41	accomplish	42	apprehend
7	arms	8	about	43	abatis	44	accommodate
9	above	10	absent	45	alternative	46	artillery
11	absurd	12	adom	47	ammunition	48	be
13	adopt	14	adore	49	bay	50	by
15	advise	16	adjust	51	best	52	but
17	adjourn	18	afford	53	buy	54	bring
19	affront	20	affair	55	boat	56	bam
21	again	22	april	57	banish	58	baker
23	agent	24	alter	59	battle	60	better
25	ally	26	any	61	beacon	62	behalf
27	appear	28	appoint	63	bitter	64	bottom
29	august	30	approve	65	bounty	66	bondage
31	arrest	32	arraign	67	barron	68	brigade
33	amuse	34	assign	69	business	70	battery
35	assume	36	attempt	71	battallion	72	british

73	camp	74	came	133	dislodge	134	dismiss
75	cost	76	corps	135	dragoon	136	detain
77	change	78	carry	137	divert	138	discourse
79	clergy	80	common	139	disband	140	dismount
81	consult	82	contest	141	disarm	142	detect
83	contract	84	content	143	defense	144	deceive
85	Congress	86	captain	145	delay	146	difficult
87	careful	88	city	147	disapprove	148	disregard
89	clamour	90	column	149	disappoint	150	disagree
91	copy	92	cover	151	disorder	152	dishonest
93	county	94	courage	153	discover	154	december
95	credit	96	custom	155	demolish	156	deliver
97	compute	98	conduct	157	desolate	158	during
99	comply	100	confine	159	ear	160	eye
101	caution	102	conquer	161	end	162	enquire
103	coward	104	confess	163	effect	164	endure
105	convict	106	cannon	165	enforce	166	engage
107	character	108	circumstance	167	enclose	168	equip
109	clothier	110	company	169	excuse	170	exert
111	confident	112	committee	171	expand	172	expose
113	continue	114	contradict	173	extort	174	express
115	correspond	116	controversy	175	embark	176	employ
117	commission	118	commissioner	177	explore	178	enemy
119	constitution	120	date	179	example	180	embassador
121	day	122	dead	181	engagement	182	experience
123	do	124	die	183	evacuate	184	Farm
125	damage	126	doctor	185	face	186	fat
127	dirty	128	drummer	187	FALSE	188	friend
129	daily	130	dispatch	189	fen	190	find
131	distant	132	danger	191	form	192	fort

193 fleet	194 famine	253 hope	254 hut
195 father	196 foggy	255 horse	256 house
197 folly	198 frugal	257 happy	258 hardy
199 faithfull	200 favour	259 harvest	260 horrid
201 faulty	202 foreign	261 horseman	262 human
203 forget	204 fulfil	263 havock	264 healthy
205 factor	206 faculty	265 heavy	266 honest
207 favorite	208 fortune	267 hunger	268 honor
209 forget	210 foreigner	269 harmony	270 hazardous
211 fortitude	212 fortify	271 hesitate	272 history
213 formidable	214 foundation	273 horrible	274 hospital
215 february	216 get	275 hurrican	276 hypocrite
217 great	218 good	277 document damage	
219 gun	220 go	278 document damage	
221 gain	222 guide	279 document damage	
223 gold	224 glory	280 I	
225 gunner	226 gloomy	281 if	282 in
227 govern	228 grandieure	283 is	284 it
229 guilty	230 guinea	285 ice	286 ink
231 gallant	232 gazette	287 into	288 instance
233 grateful	234 glacis	289 island	290 impress
235 general	236 garrison	291 improve	292 incamp
237 gentleman	238 glorious	293 incur	294 infest
239 gradual	240 grandadier	295 inforce	296 instance
241 hay	242 he	297 insnare	298 instruct
243 his	244 him	299 intrigue	300 intrust
245 haste	246 hand	301 instant	302 invest
247 hang	248 hour?	303 invite	304 ignorant
249 have	250 head	305 impudent	306 industry
251 high	252 hill	307 infamous	308 influence

309	infantry		
310	infantry (symbol)		
311	injury	312	innocent
313	instrument	314	intimate
315	illegal	316	imagin
317	important	318	imprison
319	improper	320	incumber
321	inhuman	322	inquiry
323	interview	324	incorrect
325	interceed	326	interfere
327	intermix	328	introduce
329	immediate	330	impatient
331	incouragment		
332	infection		
333	irregular	334	invalid
335	indians	336	June
337	July	338	jury
339	jealous	340	justify
341	January	342	key
343	king	344	kill
345	know	346	law
347	land	348	love
349	low	350	lot
351	lord	352	light
353	last	354	learn
355	lady	356	letter
357	levy	358	levies-new
359	liar	360	lucky
361	language	362	limit
363	liquid	364	longitude
365	latitude	366	laudable
367	legible	368	liberty
369	lottery	370	literature
371	man	372	map
373	may	374	march
375	mast	376	make
377	met	378	me
379	my	380	much
381	move	382	most
383	mine	384	many
385	mercy	386	moment
387	murder	388	measure
389	method	390	mischief
391	mistake	392	molest
393	majesty	394	meditate
395	memory	396	messenger
397	misery	398	moveable
399	multitude	400	miscarry
401	misfortune	402	miserable
403	mercenary	404	majority
405	minority	406	memorial
407	missterious	408	manufacture
409	moderator	410	ministerial
411	name	412	new
413	no	414	not
415	night	416	never
417	needful	418	number
419	neither	420	nothing
421	neglect	422	nation
423	navy	424	natural

425	negative	426	negligence
427	november	428	necessary
429	nobility	430	oath
431	of	432	off
433	on	434	or
435	out	436	offer
437	office	438	onset
439	order	440	over
441	obstruct	442	obtain
443	observe	444	occur
445	offense	446	ommit
447	oppose	448	obligate
449	obstinate	450	obviate
451	occupy	452	operate
453	origin	454	ornament
455	overcome	456	overlook
457	overtake	458	overrun
459	overthrow	460	obedience
461	objection	462	october
463	obscure	464	occasion
465	opinion	466	oppression
467	opportunity	468	obligation
469	pay	470	peace
471	plan	472	put
473	port	474	proof
475	please	476	part
477	paper	478	pardon
479	party	480	perfect
481	pilot	482	prudent
483	publish	484	purchase

485	purpose	486	people
487	pleasure	488	produce
489	prison	490	progress
491	promise	492	proper
493	prosper	494	prospect
495	punish	496	pertake
497	perform	498	permit
499	pervert	500	prepare
501	prevail	502	preserve
503	pretend	504	promote
505	propose	506	protect
507	provost	508	pursue
509	passenger	510	passion
511	pension	512	period
513	persecute	514	poverty
515	power or powerful		
516	prosperous		
517	punishment	518	preferment
519	production	520	pursuant
521	pensioner	522	Parliament
523	persecution	524	practicable
525	profitable	526	particular
527	petition	528	profession
529	proclaim	530	provision
531	protection	532	quick
533	question	534	quantity
535	quality	536	rank
537	rain	538	run
539	rule	540	read
541	rise	542	random

543	ransom	544	rather	601	silent	602	suffer
545	real	546	riot	603	sudden	604	surprise
547	robber	548	ready	605	summer	606	speaker
549	ruin	550	ruler	607	steady	608	submit
551	rapid	552	reader	609	surpass	610	sanction
553	rebel	554	rigor	611	sensible	612	singular
555	river	556	receit	613	soldier	614	sovereign
557	refit	558	regain	615	security	616	severity
559	rejoice	560	relate	617	?	618	september
561	request	562	relax	619	surrender	620	serviceable
563	redoubt	564	rely	621	security	622	severity
565	remit	566	reprieve	623	society	624	superior
567	repulse	568	reward	625	the	626	that
569	retreat	570	resign	627	this	628	these
571	ratify	572	recompense	629	they	630	there
573	regular	574	regulate	631	thing	632	though
575	rigorous	576	recital	633	time	634	to
577	recover	578	remember	635	troops	636	thankfull
579	remittance	280	represent	637	therefore	638	timber
581	rebellion	582	reduction	639	tory	640	transport
583	remarkable			641	trail	642	traitor
584	reinforcement			643	transgress	644	translate
585	refugee	586	sail	645	terrible	646	tyranny
587	see	588	sea	647	vain	648	vaunt
589	scheme	590	set	649	vouch	650	vacant
591	send	592	ship	651	vary	652	venture
593	safe	594	same	653	vital	654	vulgar
595	sky	596	secret	655	value	656	virtue
597	seldom	598	sentence	657	visit	658	valiant
599	servant	600	signal	659	victory	660	vigilant

661	vigorous	662	violent
663	volenteer	664	valuable
665	voluntary	666	up
667	upper	668	upon
669	unto	670	unarm
671	unfit	672	unheard
673	unsafe	674	uniform
675	uncertain	676	uncommon
677	unfriendly	678	unfortunate
679	wind	680	war
681	was	682	we
683	will	684	with
685	when	686	wharf
687	wound	688	wood
689	want	690	wait
691	write	692	who
693	wish	694	whose
695	wages	696	warlike
697	welfare	698	willing
699	winter	700	water
701	woman	702	writer
703	waggon	704	weary
705	warrant	706	yet
707	you	708	your
709	yesterday	710	zeal
711	Gen Washington		
712	Clinton		
713	Tryon	714	Erskind
715	Vaughan	716	Robinson
717	Brown	718	Gen Garth

719	North, Lord	720	Germain
721	Bolton, John		
722	Culper, Sam		
723	Culper, Junr.	724	Austin Roe
725	C. Brewster	726	Rivingston
727	New York	728	Long Island
729	Setauket		
730	Kingsbridge		
731	Bergen		
732	Staten Island		
733	Boston		
734	Rhode Island		
735	Connecticut	736	New Jersey
737	Pennsylvania	738	Maryland
739	Virginia		
740	North Carolina		
741	South Carolina		
742	Georgia		
743	Quebeck	744	Hallifax
745	England	746	London
747	Portsmouth	748	Plymouth
749	Ireland	750	Corke
751	Scotland	752	West Indies
753	East Indies	754	Gibralter
755	France	756	Spain
757	Scotland	758	Portugal
759	Denmark	760	Russia
761	Germany	762	Hanover
763	Head Quarters		

e	A			v	T	w	U
f	B	g	C	x	V	y	W
h	D	i	E	z	X	s	Y
j	F	a	G	t	Z	e	1
b	H	c	I	f	2	g	3
d	J	o	K	i	4	k	5
m	L	n	M	m	6	n	7
p	N	q	O	0	8	q	9
r	P	k	Q	u	0		
l	R	u	S				

Heroines and Heroes of the

Revolutionary War

WOMEN AND YOUNG GIRLS like Sybil Ludington played a very important role in helping George Washington win the Revolutionary War, although very little is said about them.

Catherine Barry — Cowpens. Have you ever heard of it? Well, it's located in South Carolina. A battle there helped bring about the end to the Revolutionary War. It was 1781. The British, under command of General Cornwallis, set out to crush a group of Patriots commanded by a General Morgan. General Morgan, realizing how out-manned he was, appealed to Catherine Moor Barry for help. She knew every square inch of the land there. She knew every shortcut and trail, where Patriots lived, and how to contact them. Single-handedly Catherine rounded up the necessary local Patriots to join General Morgan's troops. With her help, General Morgan laid a trap for General Cornwallis and his men. The plan worked. General Cornwallis was defeated, retreating into the hands of General Washington at Yorktown, Virginia. With his surrender, the colonies won their independence from Britain. Again, a woman's hand assisted Patriots in their war effort.

Esther Reed — Born in England, Esther was used to the comforts of life, but the War for Independence was in its fifth year, lasting longer than anyone had expected. She knew something had to be done. Together with other women in Philadelphia she formed The Philadelphia Association, the largest women's organization of the Revolutionary War. These women, who lived with warmth while soldiers froze in their tents, decided to take action. They raised money to give to the soldiers; however, General Washington was opposed to this plan. The two entities compromised, and the Association agreed to make warm shirts for the troops. Each shirt's maker stitched her name onto the shirt's collar. This personal touch helped raise the spirts for those receiving the gift.

Nancy Ward — Nancy witnessed her husband's death in a battle with Creek Indians. She took up his bow and arrow and led her Cherokee tribe to victory. Nancy, as Americans called her, was named "Beloved Woman" by the tribe and placed at the head of the Women's Council. She also served as a member of the Council of Chiefs.

Penelope Barker — Months before any active independence movement, Penelope led the Edenton Tea Party. Unlike the better known Boston Tea Party, Penelope and more than 50 women did not dress up in costumes to show the British how they felt. Instead she wrote a declaration against the use of tea and clothes made from British cloth. All the women at the meeting signed it. Women's opinions at the time were not considered important so naturally the British laughed at them. Before long, though, the British took notice as more women joined the boycott of British goods. Without firing a shot, these women let the British know that power lies in the hands of those who rock the boat. Women joined men in showing the British that they, too, would not stand for taxation without representation.

Anna Strong — According to widely accepted local and family tradition, Anna Strong's role in the Culper Spy Ring was to signal Brewster — who ran regular trips with whaleboats across the Sound on a variety of smuggling and military missions — that a message was ready. She did this by hanging a black petticoat on her clothesline at Strong Point in Setauket, which was easily visible by Brewster from a boat. It was also visible to Woodhull from his nearby farm after he began to operate almost exclusively from home. Anna would add a number of handkerchiefs for one of six coves where Brewster would bring his boat, and Woodhull would meet him.

Lydia Cope — I have described both Elizabeth and her daughter in the book. We don't know if Lydia was truly Agent 355. After reading many books on the subject, it is only my conjecture that she was the spy. She had a baby and died on the HMS *Jersey*. The baby's father was Robert Townsend.

Peggy Arnold — Peggy was Benedict Arnold's wife and John Andre's (the British Spy) lover. I wonder if Benedict would have become a traitor for the British if he had known his wife was the lover of his co-conspirator?

Grace and Rachel Martin — The bravery of these two women escalated when the Martin sisters grew tired of the deplorable way the British treated women and children. They sought opportunities to help. Knowing that a courier was bringing British documents to South Carolina, they set out to intercept him and retrieve the papers for the Patriots. Borrowing their husbands' clothes and pistols, they waited in the dark along the road. Upon hearing horses, they stopped the British officers and took what they came for without firing a single shot. They got quite the surprise, however, when they arrived home later that night and found the very men they had robbed in their living room enjoying a meal their mother had prepared! Luckily for them, men in the dark look different from women in the light!

Patience Wright — Have you ever been to a wax museum? Making wax sculptures of people was a popular art form in Colonial America. Patience was particularly good at it. When her wax figures couldn't take the heat due to the fires, she took a boat to England. She maintained her fondness for her "America," however. When war broke out in the colonies, Patience decided to remain in England. She pumped her patrons for information about the rebellion in the colonies and secretly hid pertinent bits in the wax figures she was so proud of. When American prisoners were taken to England for safekeeping, Patience and others helped many escape. Not one prisoner wanted to be buried in England.

Prudence Wright — Have you ever considered the idea of Minutewomen? It could happen! In fact, it did — at least on one night. While the men were out looking for British soldiers, Prudence Wright gathered the women of Groton, Massachusetts together to defend the bridge that led into town. They disguised themselves in their husbands' clothes and armed themselves with whatever they could get their hands on, including pitchforks. When a British officer's presence was given away by the sound of his horse's hooves on the bridge, the women left the safety of the reeds and relieved him of the secret messages he was carrying. The documents were passed on to the local Patriot Committee of Safety. Once home, the women laughed at the surprise of the British officer when he found out that he had been had by women.

Sybil Ludington — Sybil has been celebrated as the female Paul Revere because of her ride through Putnam and Dutchess Counties to warn the militia that British troops were burning Danbury, Connecticut. Danbury was a Patriot supply center. After burning it the British headed for Fredricksburg, New York. A young soldier arrived at Sybil's father's home. Colonel Ludington was in charge of the local volunteers. Needing someone to go at once to gather the troops, Sybil jumped at the chance. She rode to the many villages, informing everyone about what was happening. Thanks to her bravery, the Patriots were able to force the British back to Long Island Sound. From there, they boarded ship and sailed away. Chalk up another win for America's brave women!

Nancy Morgan Hart — This woman was known to have a hot temper, fearless spirit, and a quick hand to deliver revenge if she felt she or any member of her family had been harmed. The most well-known account of Nancy's life begins when six British soldiers stopped at her cabin in search of a Patriot leader, demanding information as to whether he had stopped at her farm. Although the man they were tracking had been there, she denied seeing anyone. Convinced that she was lying, one of the British soldiers shot and killed Nancy's prized turkey and ordered her to cook it for them. Entering the cabin, they stacked their weapons in a corner and demanded something to drink. Nancy obliged by serving up wine — plenty of it. As the soldiers drank, Hart sent her daughter to the spring for a bucket of water. Secretly she instructed her to blow a conch shell kept in a nearby stump to alert the neighbors that British soldiers were in the cabin. Ms. Hart served her unwelcome visitors and wove between them and their weapons, she began to pass the muskets through an opening in the cabin wall to her daughter, who had slipped outside to the rear of the house. When the soldiers noticed what was going on, they rushed to try and retrieve what weapons were left. She gave them one warning that she would shoot and kill the next man who moved. Unfortunately, one man ignored her warning, and seconds later he lay dead on the floor.

Asher Wright — Asher was a manservant of Nathan Hale and was the last American to see him alive. He described Nathan as I have in the story. One thing that is not known about Nathan was that he did not say, "Give me Liberty or give me Death." His friend Robert Tallmadge attributed it to him, but it came from a favorite author of both Robert and Nathan.

Elizabeth Burgin — She helped people escape from prison. For this she should be hanged, right? She also smuggled in food and conspired with the enemy officers — officers in the Revolutionary Army. There was a price on her head. What did she really do? Well, something quite different. There were prison ships in New York Harbor during the Revolutionary War. Ships were cheaper to build than land prisons. Elizabeth visited these prisoners as often as she could. She brought food and kindness to those retched men and women. Oh, how she wished she could do more for them. One day, a Patriot officer asked for her help in planning an escape. She brought the men information about the planned escaped, assisting over 200 prisoners. For her effort, she was forced to leave; the British wanted her dead. She escaped to New England, destitute and friendless but proud of what she had done. In 1781, Congress awarded her a pension, citing her service.

About the author

The sky is bigger, the ground harder, the freshly-grown produce amazing, and the people diversified where Linda Lee Kane lives in sunny Fresno, California.

Her family moved there with little to no expectations except to relocate back to their hometown of Huntington Beach within five years. Thirty-five years later, they have grown to love their home in the San Joaquin Valley, the people, and the opportunities that were afforded them. Linda holds a master's degree and recently retired from teaching. Her husband works at a job he loves and recently retired from coaching a semi-pro soccer team. Their two sons graduated with master's degrees and married beautiful, intelligent women.

Whether she's writing for adults or children, the war between Linda's days and nights is often reflected in her books. Although the tendency to acknowledge the light and dark sides of life is disguised in her work, it's there, lurking, just out of view. Besides the power of love, land, and sky, Linda's husband and two sons are the other major influences on her work and on her. They have served as blunt and humbling story consultants over the years to a struggling writer.

Today Linda Kane lives between the sea and the valley where she writes and edits, paints, plays with her two grandchildren and three dogs, rides and drives her Saddlebred horses and Hackney pony, and enjoys life to the fullest.

www.ingramcontent.com/pod-product-compliance
Lightning Source LLC
Chambersburg PA
CBHW031114260626
47172CB00001B/360